D0811366

60000 0000 29068

Colorado Clean-up

Provost Captain Slade Moran sets out from Fort Benson, Colorado, to investigate the disappearance of an army pay roll and its military escort.

The grim trail brings him to the empty roll coach and a murdered escort, with one soldier mysteriously missing. Captain Moran is led to Moundville where he is confronted by desperate men plotting to steal a gold mine.

In this story of double-cross and mayhem Moran fears he will fail in his duty. Against all odds, can he succeed?

By the same author

Range Grab
Bank Raid
Range Wolves
Gun Talk
Violent Trail
Lone Hand
Gunsmoke Justice
Big Trouble
Gun Peril
War at the Diamond O
Twisted Trail
Showdown at Singing Springs
Blood and Grass
The Hanna Gang
Raven's Feud
Hell Town
Faces in the Dust
Steel Tracks – Iron Men
Marshal Law
Arizona Showdown
Shoot-out at Owl Creek
The Long Trail
Running Crooked
Hell's Courtyard
Kill or Be Killed
Desperate Men
Ready for Trouble
Border Fury
Prairie Wolves
Gunslinger Breed
Violent Men

Colorado Clean-up

Corba Sunman

A Black Horse Western

ROBERT HALE · LONDON

© Corba Sunman 2011
First published in Great Britain 2011

ISBN 978-0-7090-9179-0

Robert Hale Limited
Clerkenwell House
Clerkenwell Green
London EC1R 0HT

www.halebooks.com

The right of Corba Sunman to be identified as
author of this work has been asserted by him
in accordance with the Copyright, Designs and
Patents Act 1988

Peterborough City Council	
60000 0000 29068	
Askews & Holts	Aug-2011
AF/WES	£13.25

Typeset by
Derek Doyle & Associates, Shaw Heath
Printed and bound in Great Britain by
CPI Antony Rowe, Chippenham and Eastbourne

ONE

The payroll coach with the cavalry escort had left Fort Benson at sunup and was raising dust on the trail to Colorado Springs through the hot August sunshine. A sergeant and six cavalrymen were escorting the vehicle; three troopers rode either side of the coach to avoid the worst of the dust thrown up by the churning wheels. Major Gerald Sterling, doing duty as Paymaster for the Army of the Interior, was relaxing inside the vehicle. The driver, Corporal Ryker, urged the four-horse hitch along at their best pace, following the trail that meandered through a desolate wilderness. The surrounding skyline was ragged with desolate grey peaks. There was little in the way of vegetation in this area, where the only activity by the hard men inhabiting it was digging into the ground for gold or silver.

Sergeant Tully led the escort, with orders to hand over the responsibility for the payroll to a detail of the garrison in Colorado Springs. Tully, tall and rugged, had twenty years' experience of army life in the West, and had lost count of the times he had ridden this route escorting a payroll. But today, he was more alert than usual for he had been warned of possible trouble from a gang of robbers that had stopped a Wells Fargo coach for its cash box recently and made off with wages for the miners, and there had been a bank raid six months ago in the mining town of Moundville, forty miles to the east.

But to Tully's certain knowledge, no attempt had ever been made to steal an army payroll, although he was taking no chances. He twisted in his saddle for the hundredth time in as many minutes to check on the escort, and frowned when he saw that Trooper Price was out of position. Price had ridden forward and was speaking to Corporal Ryker. Tully shouted for Price to resume his position and faced his front again, aware that he would be greatly relieved when this particular duty had ended.

The crash of a pistol shot blasted through the heavy silence and flung a string of echoes into the surrounding peaks. Tully was startled despite his alertness, and twisted once more in his saddle. He saw Corporal Ryker pitching sideways off the seat of the wagon, clutching at his chest; Price was enveloped in gun smoke. Tully reached for his pistol, his reflexes honed to a fine edge by life on the frontier. As his Army Colt came to hand, Tully saw another of the escort lean sideways and fire two shots through the side window of the coach as Price reached the lead horse and grabbed at the reins.

Tully swung his mount and lifted his pistol. More shots crashed and two of the escorting troopers pitched out of their saddles, shot down by another of the escort. Tully, shocked, wondered what the hell was going on, and then realized that one of the troopers was drawing a bead on him. He cocked his pistol, but received a terrific blow in his chest. Pain flashed through him like summer lightning. He sensed that he was falling out of his saddle but was unaware of hitting the rocky ground – he died as he vacated his saddle.

Trooper Price brought the team to a standstill. He rode back to the coach and jerked open a door. Major Sterling was dead, lying slumped across the iron-bound chest containing the payroll. Price checked the two troopers who had been shot. Parfitt was dead – Chambers was still breathing. Price fired a shot and Chambers died. Price grinned as he listened to the fading echoes of the shooting.

'I told you it would be easy,' he remarked to the three remaining troopers. 'Now look lively, boys, and let's get this wagon off the trail. We'll get paid off in Moundville and be done with it. Stick all the bodies in the coach and tie the loose horses behind. Biddle, get on the driving seat and whip up that team. We need to put distance between us and this spot. Porter, you and Lansdale start blotting our tracks. We don't want any trail left between here and Moundville.'

The troopers set to, and moments later the coach continued on its way as if nothing untoward had occurred. Only a patch of blood where Sergeant Tully had fallen remained as mute testimony to the violence that had taken place. The coach turned off the trail within a mile of the incident and disappeared into a narrow gully. As the dust settled, two of the soldiers began blotting out the faint tracks that marked the passing of the vehicle. They worked meticulously along the dry wash until they reached solid rock. Then, satisfied that they had obliterated all signs of the coach passing, they returned to the entrance to the gully and blocked it with loose rocks before hastening to overhaul the coach, which had continued to head in the direction of the distant mining town of Moundville.

Price rode ahead. He was big; thick-set, with brown eyes that were like two pieces of rock, glinting with a malevolence that permeated his mind and coloured his outlook and attitude. He had a prominent chin and a long nose. He kept glancing back at the coach and grinning as if unable to believe that he had really pulled off the robbery.

'Hey, Porter, you and Lansdale blot any tracks we leave or we'll have a patrol from the fort chasing us up before we can get clear. And put some effort into it. We'll be rid of the coach before dawn tomorrow, so keep at it.'

'We'll never make it,' Biddle called. 'This team will be dead in their tracks long before midnight.'

'We've got some spare horses tied behind the coach,' Price replied. 'We'll switch them around after another ten miles. I want to be in the high ground above Moundville before the sun shows, and the worst thing that could happen to us is being spotted before we're in the clear. The less folks around there see of us the better it will be.'

'I think we are making a mistake sticking with the coach,' said Biddle. 'It is easier to track than saddle horses. How far is it to Moundville?'

'Twenty miles as the crow flies, but it is a lot more by the route we are taking.' Price laughed. 'Don't worry. Everything is going well. We'll meet some friends along the way and they'll take over from us. Then we'll be free to ride on with five hundred bucks apiece in our pockets. I've even arranged for new clothes to be brought for us.'

'Why don't we take all the dough and split it between the four of us?' Biddle demanded. 'Why do we have to hand it over to someone else?'

Price uttered an oath as he twisted in his saddle and glared at Biddle.

'I told you when you came into this not to ask questions,' he rasped. 'The robbery was set up by a very clever man. I couldn't have handled it by myself. My part was to organize it at the army end, and we are getting well paid for an easy job. We'll hand over the coach and its contents, get our dough and then we'll disappear. Whatever happens after that, we won't be around to take the can if anything goes wrong. So stop asking questions and keep the coach moving.'

Biddle grimaced and cracked the whip. He opened his mouth to speak but changed his mind and closed it again. The coach lurched and slithered over solid rock, heading deeper and deeper into the desolate wilderness.

They continued, sometimes making slow progress but remaining unseen. Price led the way unerringly, constantly referring to a map to find the reference points he needed. They halted frequently to rest the horses, and the sun was close to the distant peaks in the west when Price saw movement ahead and reached for his gun.

'Hold it,' he called to Biddle, who hauled on the reins and brought the coach to a halt.

Three riders materialized from the grey indistinctness of the evening.

'Are they the men you are expecting to meet?' called Biddle.

'Sure.' Price grinned. 'And they are right on schedule. We're almost finished now, boys. I'll ride ahead and talk to them.'

Price touched spurs to his horse and cantered toward the newcomers, who had reined in and were sitting their mounts. Price was exultant. The most difficult part of the robbery had been accomplished. He reined in before the trio, who were grinning. They were hard-bitten men, well-armed and alert. The foremost was tall and thin, his dark features sharp, hawk-like; his blue eyes the coldest Price had ever looked into. Rafe Cullen was a killer with a string of murders stretching like milestones back through his notorious past.

'How do, Cullen?' Price said. 'Glad to see you.'

'You made good time,' Cullen responded. 'Do you know Sarn and Kenton?'

'I've seen them around Moundville.' Price nodded as he regarded the two men with Cullen. Sarn was small, hard-faced. Kenton was over-large, fleshy, with a moon face and narrowed blue eyes. Neither man greeted Price, who got the impression that they were like two mountain cats preparing to spring on unsuspecting prey.

'Did you have any trouble?' demanded Cullen.

'No. It went off OK.'

'That's good.' Cullen looked over Price's shoulder at the coach. Biddle was motionless on the driving seat. Porter and Lansdale were sitting their mounts beside the vehicle. 'There's been a change of plan, Price. Because of your brother, you'll be the only survivor of the escort. Those three men will be too dangerous to turn loose with five hundred bucks apiece in their pockets. They might be recognized, or brag about the robbery, so they are going into the hole with the rest of the escort.'

Price was shocked, and his expression changed. Cullen laughed harshly.

'Just sit tight where you are and we'll handle this,' Cullen continued. 'You can drive the coach to the spot where it will be disposed of, and then you can ride into Moundville with us. You're lucky you've got someone rooting for you in this set-up or you'd be wearing bullet holes right now. Come on, you two, let's get it done. Joe, you take care of the driver when I give the word. Hank, you kill the trooper on the right. OK, let's go.'

Price sat his horse stiffly, filled with cold shock as Cullen and his two sidekicks rode towards the coach. The trio moved unhurriedly, and reined in abreast of the leading horses of the team. Cullen spoke tersely. Price saw the quick movement of hands to pistols, and flinched when three shots hammered almost in unison. Biddle jerked and fell off the driving seat of the coach. Porter twisted and slumped in his saddle. Lansdale uttered a cry and fell over backwards, one foot pulling loose from a stirrup. He dropped to the ground with his other foot caught in a stirrup. The nervous horse reared and then tried to bolt but Cullen grabbed the reins and held it.

Cullen motioned for Price to go forward. Price breathed heavily as he did so. He held his reins in his left hand and kept his right hand close to the butt of his holstered pistol. Cullen grinned when he saw the expression on Price's face.

'You've got nothing to worry about, Price,' said Cullen. 'I told you what is gonna happen. You'll drive the coach

11

from here on in, and after we've got rid of all the evidence we'll ride on to Moundville with the payroll.'

Price swallowed the lump that had risen in his throat.

'Where do we get rid of the coach?' he asked.

'Don't worry about that.' Cullen shook his head. 'Tie your horse to the back of the coach and get up on the driving seat.' He motioned to his companions. 'Joe, Hank, put those three bodies into the coach, tie their horses behind and we'll get rolling.'

Price dismounted and tied his horse to the back of the coach. He ascended to the driving seat and picked up the reins. When the bodies had been loaded, Kenton and Sarn resumed their saddles. Cullen motioned for Price to get moving, and rode ahead of the vehicle with his tough companions while Price followed closely into the gathering shadows.

They made slower progress when darkness descended, and, when Price figured that it was too dangerous to continue, he hauled on the reins and applied the brake.

'It ain't safe to go on, Cullen,' he called. 'I nearly went over a drop back there.'

'Keep going. It ain't far now,' Cullen replied. 'There's a derelict mine ahead and we are gonna get rid of all the evidence in it. There have been half a dozen miners preparing the place, and when the coach has been dismantled and dumped in the mine the entrance will be closed up. We'll load the payroll on a mule and head for Moundville. Don't worry about a thing. It has all been taken care of.'

Price released the brake and cracked the whip. The team lunged against their collars and the vehicle continued. Cullen rode beside the lead horse. Price had no idea where they were heading, and was surprised when he suddenly saw the gleam of lanterns ahead in the darkness. They pulled into a miners' camp where half a dozen men were waiting – anonymous figures in the uncertain gloom. Price stepped down from the coach and the waiting men converged on it like locusts and began dragging out the dead soldiers.

'Your job is finished now, Price,' said Cullen. 'There's a fresh horse for you here. Your army mount will be taken into the mine and killed – not a shred of evidence will remain in the open, so transfer your gear. There's a suit of clothes for you on the fresh horse, compliments of your brother. Change out of your uniform and give it to one of the miners to dump in the mine. As soon as I've transferred the payroll to a mule we'll head for Moundville.'

Price obeyed eagerly. He changed into a store suit and stood at the head of the fresh horse, watching the work party dragging the bodies of the escort out of the coach. Cullen and his two men took charge of the iron-bound chest that contained the payroll and swiftly transferred the wads of paper money into sacks and loaded them on a mule. When Cullen was ready to leave he gave orders to Hank Kenton.

'You know what to do, Hank,' he said. 'Stick around here until the miners have finished, and when they move out you go over the entire area, blotting tracks and checking that nothing has been overlooked. You'll stay here three days to watch for anyone coming in this direction. After that you return to Moundville. Do you understand what you have to do or have I got to draw you a picture?'

'Sure, I understand,' Kenton replied, grinning. 'I've got provisions to last me a week. What do I do if anyone does show up?'

'Nothing, if you can get away with it. You just see who comes, and report to me in Moundville. Just don't get seen, that's all.'

'OK. I got it. I'll see you back in town.' Kenton began to unsaddle his horse.

Cullen motioned to Price to follow and led the way out of the camp. Sarn followed him closely, leading the mule. Price looked back as he rode into the surrounding darkness, and saw the work party attacking the coach; taking it apart and toting the pieces into the adjacent mine entrance. He faced his front and followed Cullen into the night.

A sense of uneasiness gripped Ward Price as they continued. He was shocked by the callous way Biddle, Porter and Lansdale had been killed. But he was aware that dead men told no tales, and began to wonder if Cullen had the same fate planned for him, despite his brother's participation behind the scenes. He eased his pistol in his holster; although he knew he was no match for Cullen, he would fight to stay alive. He began to wish he was safely at Floyd's house in Moundville. His brother, Floyd Price, was the general manager of Big Bonanza, the largest gold mine in the area, which was owned by Royston Talmadge, a Chicago businessman who had his sticky fingers in innumerable pies and was not above using questionable measures to maintain profit margins.

Ward Price had ridden regularly to Moundville from Fort Benson to visit with his brother, and over several

months they had plotted the payroll robbery. But Floyd
had played his cards close to his chest, only hinting that
there were other, more powerful men behind him in the
steal, and he had promised Price a good new life if he
deserted the army and lifted the payroll. Now the deed was
done, and Price realized that he had burned his boats
behind him. There was no way back with murder and
robbery having been committed. A noose around his neck
was a certainty if he ever fell into the hands of the army.

It was close to midnight when Price spotted the lights of
Moundville in the distance. He felt easier now, aware that
Cullen would have killed him long before if that had been
the plan. So he was in the clear, and that new life Floyd
had promised was now at hand. He was free of the army,
which he hated, and would soon have plenty of money to
spend.

'Dismount and go to Floyd's house now,' Cullen said
when they reached the outskirts of the town. 'I'll put your
horse in the livery barn. Don't attract attention to yourself
while you are in Moundville, and give a lot of space to any
soldiers you might see. Don't plan on sticking around here
too long. The army will leave no stone unturned when
they investigate the robbery.'

'What are you gonna do with the dough?' Price
demanded.

Cullen laughed harshly. 'Don't worry about that. Like I
said, everything is taken care of. The dough will be put in
a safe place. Now get going, and don't get spotted around
town. Keep to the shadows.'

Price nodded, aware of the dangers. Moundville was
fairly close to Fort Benson. But he had no intention of

remaining. He wanted his money, and planned to lose himself where there was no chance of being recognized.

There were very few lights showing in the town as he walked along the main street but he kept to the shadows until he reached Floyd's house on the northern outskirts, which was set apart from the huddle of miners' houses at the foot of the high ground beyond the town. The mine manager's house was halfway between the main street and the entrance to the Big Bonanza mine higher up the hill. A light was showing in a downstairs window of the house, and Price heaved a long sigh of relief as he knocked at the front door. He realized that his nerves had screwed into a tight ball from the moment he had shot Corporal Ryker, the coach driver, but now he was slipping down from that impossibly high peak of tension and alertness.

The door was opened quietly and a shadowed face peered out at him. Dim light issued through the aperture, enabling him to see and be seen. He recognized his brother Floyd, who reached out a long arm, grasped his shoulder and pulled him into the house, slapping his back cordially.

'Ward, it's good to see you.' Floyd Price was tall and heavily built, fleshy from good living. 'How did it go? I've been living on my nerves all day. Did you meet up with Cullen? Is everything taken care of?'

'Yeah, it all went off OK. You sound like you're worried, Floyd. You should have been in my boots. I could sure do with a drink before I tell you what happened. But it went off like clockwork, just as we planned, and Cullen took over when we met.'

'Come into my study. You can have all the drink you

16

want. So we got the payroll. How much dough is there, do you know?'

'I've got no idea! I never saw a single bill. Cullen took charge of it. I guess you know where he's taking it, huh?'

'It will be well hidden until we need it. I knew you could do it, Ward. We planned it right down to the last detail.'

'I'm not happy about some of the things that occurred,' Ward said as he followed Floyd into a book-lined study. But the robbery was already beginning to feel like a bad dream, and he hoped a couple of drinks would blur the stark images in his mind.

'Tell me about them.' Floyd crossed to a tall window and pulled down a blind. He went to a desk where a selection of bottles was standing on a tray and poured whiskey into two glasses. He grinned as he handed a glass to Ward. 'Here's to the future, Ward. Are you aware that you have to get away from here as soon as possible? I expect the army will be buzzing around like flies on a dead coyote when they do get moving. Are you sure you left no tracks at the scene?'

'Don't worry; it went off as planned. I want to talk to you about my cut.' Ward gulped his whiskey and held out the empty glass for a refill.

'You're not satisfied with what we decided?' Floyd refilled the glass.

'The first thing Cullen did when he met us was shoot down my three pards who came into the robbery with me. That wasn't a part of the deal. Those three were good friends. We went through a lot together in the army, and I had to stand by and watch them get slaughtered.'

'You can have their share as well as your own.' Floyd set

down his glass. 'That'll give you two thousand bucks, and it should keep you going for a few months. I told you the stolen money will set us up in our new business, and in a few months you'll have a great deal of money to spend.'

'That's what you said, but I wanta know who else is in this deal with you. I'm the one who took all the risks, and I'll get my neck stretched if the army ever catches up with me. I thought you were the top man, Floyd, but that ain't so, huh?'

'I never said I was running this.' Floyd shook his head. He clapped a hand on Ward's shoulder. 'You don't need to know what is going on in the background, Ward. That knowledge could be dangerous. All you need to worry about is getting your hands on the big money that will be coming to you later.'

'What kind of business are you going into? Is it legal?'

'Look, why don't you finish your drink and go to bed? I expect you are exhausted, and a good night's sleep will set you up. We'll have a chat in the morning before I go up to the mine. But promise me you'll stay here in the house until we see what turns up when the army starts its investigation. There are folks in town who know I have a brother who is in the army, and we don't want that fact to become generally known. You can have your two thousand dollars tomorrow, so why don't you slip back east and have a good time? You can let me know if you need any more dough later. When the heat of the robbery dies down you'll be able to come back and join me in the gold-mining business.'

Ward drained his glass, and when he reached for the whiskey bottle Floyd reached out and grasped his wrist.

'Don't drink too much of that stuff right now,' Floyd warned. 'You'll need a clear head for a couple of weeks at least. Once you get clear of this area the sky's the limit. Now get some sleep. You know where your room is. I've got to finish some reports for Royston Talmadge, the big boss. He's due here from Chicago some time this week and I shan't have a moment to myself when he docs show up. He doesn't ever miss a trick, and he's sure got more than his share of crooked deals up his sleeve.'

Ward nodded and left the study to go to the room he used when in Moundville. He was suddenly feeling very tired, and went quickly to bed, but could not sleep initially. Bad thoughts revolved in his brain as if he had a fever. He was wary of Rafe Cullen, and wondered where the killer had taken the payroll. He tossed and turned, and, despite his near-exhaustion, the night sky was greying before he eventually slipped into the blissful realm of perfect sleep. . . .

Cullen remained hidden until Ward Price disappeared into the shadows along the street before motioning for Sarn to move on.

'Put the horses in the corral behind the livery,' Cullen instructed Sarn, 'and then head for the cabin. I'll see you there shortly.'

'What are you gonna do with all that dough?' Sarn asked.

'You know better than to ask questions,' Cullen rasped. 'Make sure you're not seen. I'll catch up with you when I get through.'

Sarn shrugged and took the reins of the restless horses. Cullen waited until Sarn was lost in the shadows around the livery barn before leading the mule to the back lots. He reached the rear of the bank and tethered the mule to a post by the back door. The bank was in total darkness. Cullen rapped on the door, which was opened almost immediately.

'Is that you, Cullen?' a hoarse voice demanded from the deep shadows.

'Who else would it be at this time of the night?' Cullen responded. 'I've got the dough. Give me a hand with these sacks.'

The payroll was carried into the bank in complete darkness. Cullen entered with the final sack and the back door was closed. A match scraped and a lamp flared into yellow light. Cullen gazed at the short, fleshy figure of Willard Bodeen, the banker. Bodeen was in his middle fifties. He was sweating profusely. Cullen laughed softly because Bodeen was tense and nervous.

'What are you getting het up about?' Cullen demanded.

'It's all right for you,' Bodeen replied hoarsely. 'Your job is finished, but I shall have this stolen money in the bank, and I'll have no explanation for its presence if it is traced here.'

'It can't be traced,' Cullen said. 'It'll be safe. Count it now and give me a receipt.'

He watched silently while Bodeen emptied the sacks and counted the money.

'I make it thirty eight thousand dollars,' Cullen said, counting with Bodeen.

Bodeen nodded and signed a receipt. Cullen departed to take the mule to the livery barn. Bodeen closed the back door of the bank with a sigh of relief and shot home the bolts. The payroll, like the coach and escort, had disappeared without a trace.

TWO

Provost Captain Slade Moran rode into Fort Benson in Colorado with orders to investigate the disappearance of the army payroll and its entire escort. Apparently, money and soldiers had disappeared without a trace and, in the three days since the incident, no evidence of what occurred had been found by the patrols sent out from Fort Benson. Moran, tall in the saddle of his buckskin, heaved a sigh of relief as he returned the salute of the sentry at the gate and rode into the fort. His pale blue eyes narrowed against the glare of the sun as he looked around the military post. He had been stationed there ten years before as a troop commander, and well remembered the harsh life of a soldier on the western frontier.

He had been on furlough, visiting his mother in Colorado Springs, when he was acquainted with the facts of the case, and had ridden immediately to Fort Benson.

A trooper on duty at the door of the headquarters' hut came forward to take the reins of the buckskin as Moran dismounted.

'Captain Moran, it's good to see you again, sir!'

Moran looked closely at the smiling trooper and recognized him.

'Sergeant Johnson,' he observed. 'Say, what happened to your stripes?'

Trooper Johnson grimaced. 'I'm happier in the ranks, Captain,' he replied.

Moran nodded, recalling that Johnson had a weakness for whiskey. Moran was wearing a light blue town suit instead of his uniform. He stretched and breathed deeply as he relaxed. Three inches over six feet in height, broad-shouldered and lean at the waist, his bronzed face proclaimed that he was an outdoor type and his blue eyes were far-seeing. He was thirty years old and well versed in military law. A cartridge belt showed under his open jacket; the holster contained a .45 Army Model Colt.

'Is Major Rogers in his office, Johnson?' Moran said.

'He is, sir. Will you be riding out again soon?'

'As soon as possible,' Moran replied.

He entered the company office. Top Sergeant Giddings sprang to his feet behind a desk and saluted. Giddings had been Moran's troop sergeant ten years before. He had put on a considerable amount of weight since taking over the administration of B Troop and his sparse, cropped hair was now iron-grey.

'Captain Moran,' the non-com greeted. 'It's a pleasure to see you, sir. The major is expecting you. We had a wire saying you would be handling the case, but we didn't expect to see you so soon. Please step this way, sir.'

'How are you doing, Giddings?' Moran asked. 'Nothing seems to have changed around here since I left.'

'That's a fact, sir. It must be all of ten years now,

Captain.' Giddings smiled broadly. 'Time has a habit of seeming to stand still out here. It is only us poor humans who feel the effects of its passing.'

Giddings tapped at the commanding officer's door and opened it. He announced Moran, who entered the inner office and saluted the major seated at a desk by a window which overlooked the parade ground. Major Rogers was in his early forties; immaculately dressed in his blue uniform with its yellow cavalry markings. They exchanged salutes, and Rogers got to his feet. He was not as tall as Moran, but carried more weight, and although he smiled a greeting, his face was set in a serious expression that no amount of relaxation could erase. His dark eyes seemed over-bright with worry.

'Thank God you've arrived, Captain,' Rogers said. 'I'll be greatly relieved to put this business into your hands. I've had patrols out covering every inch of the trail to Colorado Springs and they've found absolutely no sign of the Paymaster, his coach, the payroll or the escort of a sergeant and six troopers. They apparently vanished into thin air. My patrols are visiting all communities in the area, but so far without success. No one, but no one, has reported seeing hide or hair of the detail. Headquarters are hammering me with demands for results, and I'm at the end of my rope trying to discover what happened. On the face of it, it is impossible for nine men, together with a coach and the payroll, to disappear without a trace, but that is exactly what has happened.'

'I'll need to talk to the patrol commanders before I take to the trail,' Moran said, 'and I'll want to look at all patrol reports from the moment the payroll detail went missing.'

Major Rogers leaned back in his seat. 'I rode out with one of the patrols because I suspected that they were not doing their job properly, but I could find no sign of what happened out there, and I have a nasty feeling that we'll never get to the bottom of it. But you go ahead with your investigation, Captain. I'll help in any way I can. My men are at your command, and I sure hope you'll be able to come up with something.'

'Thank you, Major. I'll get to work immediately.'

'Top Sergeant Giddings will assist you. Just tell him what you want and whom you wish to see and he will handle it. Keep me informed of your progress, Captain. Between us, we shall leave no stone unturned. The sooner we unravel this mystery the better.'

Moran saluted. He went back to Giddings, who was conversing with a lieutenant.

'Captain Moran, this is Lieutenant Carter,' Giddings introduced. 'The lieutenant took out the first patrol to search for the missing detail, sir.'

Carter saluted. He was tall and lean, bronzed and rugged and looked older than his twenty-four years. His dark eyes showed pleasure as he regarded Moran.

'I'm pleased to meet you, Captain. Thank God they've sent someone to look into this business. We've been running ourselves ragged trying to discover what happened, but without success. I came back yesterday from a patrol which was a complete waste of time. We located the spot where the payroll coach vanished, and carried out a meticulous sweep in all directions without finding a single clue as to what might have happened. It looked like the ground opened up, swallowed the detail, coach, horses and all and then closed over again. We never found a wheel mark or a hoof print beyond the point where the last tracks of the coach showed.'

'I shall want to leave at first light in the morning to follow the route taken by the payroll coach,' Moran said. 'You will accompany me, Lieutenant, with a detail of six troopers and, as I don't believe the payroll detail vanished into thin air, we shall take steps to discover what really happened on the trail to Colorado Springs. It may take us a great deal of time, but we will find that coach, or evidence of what happened to it.'

'Yes, sir! We'll be ready to leave at sunup, Captain.' Lieutenant Carter saluted and departed, smiling at Moran's confidence.

Moran turned to Giddings. 'I want a complete run-down on the payroll detail, Sergeant Major; a list of names and the service records of every man, and all patrol reports.'

'I have everything ready for your attention, Captain.' Giddings picked up a folder from his desk. 'I'll show you to your quarters now, sir. Trooper Davis has been assigned to you, and if there's anything you want, sir, just send Davis to me.'

Moran nodded and followed the non-com to a room in the officers' quarters. Giddings departed. Moran sat down to study the contents of the folder, until a knock at the door interrupted him. Trooper Davis entered, carrying Moran's saddle-bags and Spencer carbine.

Davis, a short, stocky man with a cheerful face and wide blue eyes, saluted and began to unpack Moran's saddle-bags.

'Just take out what I shall need until tomorrow morning,' said Moran. 'I'll be leaving at sunup with a patrol.'

'Yes, Captain. So you're going to solve this mystery, sir?'

'I hope so.' Moran glanced at the list of names of the missing detail. 'Do you know any of the men who escorted the detail?'

'All of them, sir.'

'Were you friendly with anyone in particular?'

'I knew Trooper Biddle, sir. We go back a long way. In fact I should have been on the payroll detail with him – we volunteered together for the duty, but I was replaced at the last minute.'

'Who replaced you, and why?'

'Trooper Price, sir, and I don't know why. I wasn't pleased, sir, because Biddle and me, we always look out for each other.'

'Tell Top Sergeant Giddings I want to see him immediately.'

'Yes, sir.' Davis saluted and departed.

Moran looked up Trooper Ward Price's service record, which was nothing out of the ordinary. Price had been in the army eight years and was a good soldier. He had performed his duties well and there were no crimes against his name.

Trooper Davis returned with Top Sergeant Giddings.

'Davis tells me he was taken off the payroll detail at the last minute and replaced with Trooper Price,' Moran said. 'Why was the exchange made?'

'As I remember, Captain,' Giddings replied, 'Davis was late on parade.'

Moran turned his keen blue eyes on Davis. 'Why were you late on parade that morning, Davis?'

'I was on KP duty with Trooper Hunn, sir, peeling potatoes, and Hunn accidentally cut an artery. I stopped the bleeding and took him to the doctor. By the time I got away I was late for parade, and Price had replaced me.'

Moran was satisfied with the explanation.

'That will be all for now,' he said.

'What do you think happened to the payroll, Captain?' Giddings asked.

Moran shook his head. 'I'm not in the business of making guesses,' he replied. 'I'm here to investigate the incident, and I have to start at the beginning and work through all the evidence for clues, however small they may be. At the moment there is nothing at all to go on, so I have to search through the service records of the men involved for any pointer that might throw some light on what might have happened. Generally, looking at the situation, I don't think the payroll was attacked by robbers because there were no bodies found at the spot where an attack might have taken place, and the robbers would not have taken dead soldiers along with the payroll. That's the only surmise I am prepared to make at this time.'

'Do you think it was an inside job by the military escort, sir?' Giddings persisted.

Moran shook his head. 'I'll keep an open mind until I've covered the route taken by the detachment, and then I'll look at the possibilities.'

'I hope you'll have more luck than our patrols have had,' Giddings said as he departed.

Moran did not believe in luck. He started looking

through the folder Giddings had given him; reading patrol reports and studying the service records of the payroll detail. He found nothing amiss and no clues to indicate the direction his investigation should take. He put the folder aside and summoned Trooper Davis.

'No luck yet, sir?' Davis inquired, glancing at the discarded folder.

'Not yet,' Moran replied. 'What you know about the men on the payroll detail?'

'What sort of things do you want to know, sir?'

'What they were like. Service records reveal nothing of a man's character; his likes and dislikes; if he did or did not get along in the army. Can you think of anything that might throw some light on how any of the men might have reacted to temptation?'

'Tempted to steal the payroll, Captain?' Davis grimaced. 'Maybe a couple of the men might have been, but there was a sergeant and six troopers in the detail, and not all of them would have been like-minded. Sergeant Tully commanded the escort, sir, and I've never known a more upright soldier than Tully. He lived by the book; and something like stealing a payroll just wouldn't enter his head.'

'I wouldn't look for more than two or three of the detail to be tempted,' Moran observed. 'They could have taken the rest of the escort by surprise, murdered them and made off with the coach.'

Davis gazed at Moran in shock. 'Is that what you think happened, sir?' he gasped.

'I'm merely looking at the possibilities,' Moran replied. 'The whole detail apparently vanished into thin air and, as that is impossible, then I must look elsewhere for a solution. The obvious conclusion is to suspect some of the escort until they can be eliminated.'

'There was no one on that detail I would think capable of doing such a thing, Captain.' Davis shook his head emphatically. 'I was supposed to have ridden with them, and most of us have been together for years. If someone had decided to lift the payroll, as you suspect, then they needed to do a lot of planning to pull it off, and I didn't see anyone going into a dark corner to talk about it. I certainly wasn't approached to take part in such an action. Neither was my friend Biddle or he would have mentioned it to me. I think you're barking up the wrong tree, Captain.'

Moran nodded. 'I'm merely looking at the possibilities, Davis. If the payroll was taken by some members of the escort then there are other questions which have to be considered. For instance; who was in on the steal? Where have they taken the coach? What happened to the soldiers who were not in on the heist?'

'I see what you mean, sir.' Davis grimaced. 'I'm sorry I can't be of much help, Captain, but all I can tell you is that Trooper Biddle was looking forward to getting out of the army in a couple of months. He was planning to marry and settle down in Moundville with a girl he'd met there. Her name is Dora Harmon, sir, and her father owns the store in town.'

'Moundville,' Moran mused. 'I visited it several times when I was stationed here. It's about forty miles from the fort. It used to be just a collection of miners' huts in those days, but I expect it has grown considerably in the last ten years.'

'It has, sir. It's still only a mining town, but a big mining company took over the operation of the largest mine, Big Bonanza. The last time I was there with Biddle I heard talk that the gold was petering out and some miners have already upped stakes and moved on.'

'That's the way it goes in mining communities,' Moran observed. 'OK, Davis. That will do for now. I'll want you to ride with me tomorrow. We'll be leaving at sunup.'

Davis saluted and departed. Moran left the quarters to take a stroll around the fort, noting that few changes had occurred since he was last on the post. He returned to his quarters aware that tomorrow would be a hard day, but was eager to start his investigation.

A bugle blowing reveille awoke Moran, and he was ready at first light to depart with Lieutenant Carter's patrol. He inspected the six troopers detailed to accompany him, one of them being Trooper Davis, and nodded at the alert Lieutenant Carter, who took the lead as they left the fort. Moran rode in beside Carter and they proceeded at the trot.

It was late afternoon when Carter reined in on the lonely trail to Colorado Springs and pointed to a dried bloodstain on the ground. The troopers reined in to one side. Moran stepped down from his saddle.

'This bloodstain is the only sign that something bad happened,' said Carter. 'It is four days now since the payroll coach disappeared, and there has been some traffic along here since. I was turned out immediately the coach was missed – it didn't arrive at Colorado Springs and they wired us – but I found nothing.'

'This isn't good country for tracking,' Moran observed.

'We can assume that the coach turned off the trail some-where close.' He paused to consider for a moment, and then added, 'Unless it was turned around and taken back to a turn-off.'

'I never thought of that.' Lieutenant Carter shook his head, but his tone suggested to Moran that he thought otherwise.

'It is something to consider, but we'll assume that, what-ever happened here, the coach went on to turn off later. You said the coach seemed to disappear into thin air.' Moran studied the trail. He walked back a dozen yards and then went forward again, passing the bloodstain and con-tinuing for many yards. 'The coach didn't disappear,' he mused. 'The tracks did. They've been blotted. Someone took a lot of trouble to wipe out all tracks. There's very little dust along here, so let us see how far the blotting was carried on.'

Moran walked along the trail, head bent forward; eyes studying the ground intently. He paused at times and sub-jected the ground on either side of the trail to an intense scrutiny. Lieutenant Carter followed him, shaking his head. They covered half a mile before the dust thickened again across the trail. Moran halted and turned to study the surrounding area.

'The trail between here and the bloodstain was swept continuously,' Moran mused. 'So the coach turned off somewhere along here.'

'I've been watching the ground on either side of the trail and there isn't a turn-off wide enough for a coach to pass along,' Carter said.

Moran glanced at the sky and judged that they had

another hour before sundown.

'It is too late now to do anything. Better get the men to make camp and settle down for the night, Lieutenant. I noticed a gully several yards back that looked like it might permit a coach to pass through, but there was a pile of rocks blocking the entrance.'

'I looked into it when we passed,' Carter replied, 'and it crossed my mind that it would have been a good idea to take the coach through and then move rocks into the entrance.'

Moran nodded. They retraced their steps to where a large scattering of rocks blocked the entrance to a gully. Carter walked around the rocks to check the dry wash. Moran examined the rocks. He noticed that some were of a darker grey than others, and frowned until he glanced at adjacent rocks and saw that most were of the same uniform grey.

'Lieutenant,' he called, and Carter came back to him. 'Look at these rocks. Some are light grey, like all the others around here, but some are of a darker shade. What do you make of that?'

Carter studied the pile of rocks, grimaced, and then shook his head. 'I don't know, Captain,' he said at length. 'I can't even begin to guess. What do you think?'

'The rocks have been moved into the entrance here, probably from that ledge up there. I suspect they were rolled down the slope, and these lighter grey ones came to rest in the same position as when they were up on the ledge. The darker grey ones have stopped the other way up.'

As he spoke, Moran pulled a rock away from the pile.

When he examined it he found that the side which had been facing the sun had faded to a lighter grey and the shaded side was darker. He nodded and climbed up to the ledge some twelve feet above his head to examine more rocks, and discovered that all surfaces facing the sun had been faded by countless years of relentless glare. Carter joined him, and grinned at what he saw for himself.

'It looks like someone has been too clever, Captain,' he observed. 'But it needed an experienced eye to pick up on that. So the coach and escort didn't vanish into thin air! It passed through here and then the entrance was blocked. It begins to look like someone in the escort has been guilty of failing to do his duty.'

'I'll tell you more about that when we find the coach,' Moran said. He glanced at the reddening sky, and moistened his dry lips. 'We'll check out this gully in the morning. Get the men into camp now. I'll want to hit the trail at first light.'

'It looks promising, Captain,' Carter observed. 'But I'm wondering exactly what happened here.'

'We'll discover what occurred,' Moran said. 'All we have to do is locate the coach.'

Carter laughed cynically. 'We'll likely find the coach but I'll be surprised if we ever see any trace of the payroll, sir.'

Moran nodded. He was of the same opinion. . . .

THREE

Ward Price slept and lazed through his first two days in Moundville, staying in the confines of Floyd's house and relaxing to recover from the ordeal through which he had put himself. On the third day he awoke at noon, and was surprised when he saw the sun high in the brassy sky. He peered out of the bedroom window and studied the main street, half expecting to see a patrol of soldiers from the fort already trying to trace the payroll. He grinned at the thought. It was done! He had grabbed the payroll without trouble. He guessed the robbery had been discovered by now, but he was free of the army, and would soon have an unlimited supply of money to spend. He dressed and went down to the kitchen, calling for Floyd, but the house was deserted, and he assumed that his brother had gone up to the mine.

A regular thudding sound in the background irritated him with its monotony, as it had on the previous two mornings, and he went to the back of the house and peered up at the Big Bonanza gold mine. Stark peaks reared up all around the horizon. He studied the mine workings high above; its stamp mills in the foreground ceaselessly pounding gold ore. Midway between the mine and Floyd's house stood a larger house belonging to Royston Talmadge, the owner of Big Bonanza.

Ward wandered around the house, peering out of the windows. He was averse to showing himself on the street, aware that the army would certainly turn up within a week, searching for the coach and the missing escort. He knew it was common sense to maintain a low profile, so he helped himself to some good whiskey from Floyd's ample store, and then ate breakfast.

Later, time began to hang heavily on his hands and he stood by a window overlooking the street to watch the ebb and flow of town life. This was his third day of enforced inactivity, and although he had enjoyed the first two days he could feel the first tenuous pangs of boredom assailing his mind. He had not received one red cent of his share of the robbery yet, and did not trust Floyd completely, but he controlled his impatience and went back to watching the main street for a first glimpse of military uniforms, knowing they would inevitably turn up but hoping he would not see them riding in yet. His thoughts took him back over the robbery and he tried to find fault with it, but nothing had gone wrong and he had made no mistakes.

He was jolted back to alertness when heavy knuckles hammered on the front door. He peered furtively around a curtain covering a window adjacent to the door and saw Rafe Cullen standing outside, glancing around at the street. Price grimaced at sight of the gunman. He unlocked the door and opened it a fraction. Cullen swung round to face him, and then pushed his way into the house.

'I'm glad to see you taking no chances,' Cullen growled. 'While you are in town you've got to lie low. Floyd told me to drop in on you to see how you're doing.' He reached into his pocket, withdrew a wad of notes and thrust them at Price. 'Here's your take from the robbery. It includes the share of the three soldiers we had to kill.'

Ward grabbed the money and rifled through it, his lips moving noiselessly as he counted it. Cullen watched him intently, his hard face expressionless.

'That's just a down payment, as I understand it,' Cullen observed. 'You're gonna be a partner in the new business that'll be opened up shortly, and then the sky will be the limit.'

'Floyd hasn't told me anything about the new business.' Ward stuffed the money into an inside pocket of his jacket. 'What he does now is up to him. I've finished my part in the steal, and I can't wait to pull out to where there are some bright lights.'

Cullen grinned and departed. He paused just outside the door and looked back into Ward's eyes.

'Stay under cover,' he warned. 'We want everyone to think you disappeared with the rest of the army escort, OK?'

'Sure thing.' Ward watched the gunman walk away along the street. A shiver passed through him when he saw Cullen pause and glance back at the house. He didn't trust Cullen. There was something uncanny about the killer that prickled in his mind, and he was relieved that he would not be spending too much time around here. The bright lights were beckoning, and he couldn't wait to shake the dust of Moundville off his boots. He had thrown off his military shackles, burned his bridges behind him and meant to have himself a high old time.

Floyd Price was at the Big Bonanza mine before the sun had barely cleared the eastern horizon. He was expecting Royston Talmadge to show up some time during the day, but he was more interested in seeing Kerry Talmadge, Royston's only son, whose original idea it was to rob his father of the Big Bonanza. Now the payroll had been stolen it was time to take the next step forward in the big steal they had planned. Floyd was not happy using Kerry Talmadge, for the youngster was a wilful pleasure-seeker with a number of character weaknesses that boded ill for anyone attempting to make use of him. But Floyd was desperate, and overlooked the fact that Kerry probably did not have the stomach to go all the way along the crooked trail to reap the great wealth which they had evolved. Kerry was the only man who could carry off the deception needed to drop Big Bonanza into their hands like a ripe apple falling from a tree. As the spoiled and wilful only son of Royston Talmadge, Kerry was the only man in the world who might get away with deceiving his father.

Hal Dano, Floyd's assistant, was already in the office when Floyd entered. Dano was energetic and full of business; a fresh-faced young man trained as a geologist who was always eager to please Floyd, it had taken Floyd a long time to get Dano to join him in the big deception. It would have been impossible for Floyd to swing the deal without Dano being aware of what was going on, so Dano had been enticed. But Floyd was not completely sure of Dano yet, and when he saw a troubled expression on his assistant's face he immediately feared the worst.

'What's bothering you, Hal?' Floyd demanded. 'Not getting cold feet, are you?'

Dano's blue eyes narrowed. 'I saw Kerry Talmadge in the hotel last night. He came in from Denver ahead of Royston, who is due today, and Kerry was the worse for whiskey. He was in the company of that two-bit gunnie who acts as his bodyguard. I heard Kerry's tongue running out of control, like it always does when he's had a couple of drinks too many, and he was saying things that he should have kept to himself if we are to pull off this crooked deal. You'll have to stop his mouth, Floyd. You know I was never confident we could pull this off, but with a broken reed like Kerry in the game it sure looks like we are heading along the trail to disaster.'

Floyd grimaced. 'I wish Kerry would stay in the background. He doesn't need to get involved personally, but he wants to get at his father any way he can. I don't believe his attitude half the time. Royston has given Kerry everything he has ever asked for, and more, and if it were me I'd worship the ground the old man walks on, but not Kerry. He hates his father, and will do anything short of murder to put one over on him. I'd better get along to the hotel and talk to him. If I can't make him pull in his horns then the whole deal is off.'

'Haven't we passed the point of no return?' Dano asked.

'You know that and I know that.' Floyd compressed his lips. 'But Kerry doesn't. I'll try to head him off.'

'It will be as useless as standing in front of a runaway train to stop it,' Dano observed.

'So do you have a better idea?' Floyd countered.

Dano shrugged. 'If I was running this deal I'd get someone to put a slug through Kerry's stupid head. It's the only way you can be sure of silencing him.'

Floyd laughed harshly. 'You've certainly changed your way of thinking, Hal.'

'Murder has already been done.' Dano spoke through clenched teeth. 'The cavalry escort with the payroll coach.'

'Yeah, that's the only bit in the scheme I don't like to think about. But there was no other way, and it is done now. There's no going back from here. We go on no matter what happens, and if Kerry is asking to collect a bullet then he'll get one right where he can't digest it. Stay on your toes this morning, Hal, in case Royston drops in on us suddenly. He's fond of doing that. You never know which way he's gonna jump. He's like a cat on hot bricks when it comes to business. I'll go down to the hotel to see Kerry. If Royston does show up before I get back, then tell him I've gone into the mine to sort out a problem.'

Dano nodded, his expression showing that he was far from happy.

Floyd went back to town. He needed to see how Willard Bodeen, the banker, was getting on with the stolen payroll in his safe. Bodeen was another in the plan who gave him cause for disquiet, but he had to use the best men available, and was prepared to drop anyone who didn't measure up. His thoughts were fast and furious as he walked to the hotel. He had done well to bring in all the men he needed to carry off his deception successfully, and Bodeen had been the most difficult to convince, until a bank robbery had left him needing cash urgently and convinced him that Floyd's scheme was a lifesaver.

It was still early when Floyd entered the hotel, which was the tallest building in Moundville; three storeys high with twenty bedrooms. The first man he saw was Cass Frint, Kerry's pet gunman, who was standing beside the reception desk chatting to the hotel clerk. Frint had been born in the back streets of Chicago and grew up thinking that crime was the only worthwhile occupation in the whole world. Tall, and thin, he was not physically strong, but inordinately fast and accurate with a pistol, and not bothered by conscience. He had saved Kerry Taldmadge's life some years before and, because of his gun skill and close mouth, had become Kerry's closest companion.

'Howdy, Floyd,' greeted Frint. His brown eyes seemed lifeless. His voice was flat and quiet, but held an under-current of menace. 'Are you looking for Kerry?'

'Is he up and about yet?'

'Nope. And don't expect to see him this side of noon. He sure tied one on last night. Old man Talmadge will be turning up pretty soon and it won't do if he catches Kerry still in bed.'

'So go and drag Kerry out of his sack,' Floyd suggested.

'You know better than that.' Frint's eyes turned bleak. 'What are you trying to do – drop me in it? I'd be out of a job if I pulled a stunt like that.'

'OK. When you do see Kerry, tell him I was here and I need to see him urgently. I've got some other business to handle right now so I'll come back shortly.'

Floyd turned and looked into the dining room; he saw it was practically deserted, and entered to have breakfast. He knew that by the time he had eaten, Willard Bodeen would be at his desk in the bank. He considered his plan while he ate, and could not fault any detail. When he left the hotel he noticed that the blind in Bodeen's office in the bank was raised and went across the street.

Bodeen was seated behind his desk, Floyd judged that the banker seemed to be in a highly nervous state. He did not like what he saw.

'What's wrong, Will?' he demanded. 'Is something bothering you?'

'I don't like having that stolen payroll in the bank,' Bodeen replied.

'So what are you het up about? Don't get cold feet. We've got the dough so we are in this right up to our necks, and there is only one way to go from here, which is forward. All you've got to do is hold on to the payroll until we need it. Where's the risk in that? It's only money, and one dollar bill looks just like another, huh? A bank is supposed to have plenty of dough around, isn't it? Just cool down, Will, and hang on to your nerve. You've got nothing to worry about, and when we get through this you'll have a helluva lot more dough lying around in here.'

'I'm holding on,' Bodeen replied. 'But if an auditor shows up and I have money in the safe that I can't account for, it will be all up with me.'

'You worry too much,' Floyd said roughly. 'What the hell, Will! If you are that scared then take the dough out after dark and bury it on the back lot. Don't lose any sweat over this. Pull yourself together. I've got enough on my mind now without having to think about you. It is getting close to the time when I've got to make my first move, and how far do you think I'd get if I let nerves get the better of me?'

'I'm having second thoughts about this business, Floyd,' Bodeen said harshly. 'I wish I hadn't become involved.'

'That's too bad. You came in, and now you'll have to stick with it. You'll take your share of what we get, won't you? OK. So settle down and keep your mind on what you have to do.'

Bodeen shook his head. Floyd departed, wondering if his carefully laid plans were beginning to disintegrate. But as far as he was concerned the worst of it was over, and apart from one or two small points to be taken care of there was nothing that could go wrong. All he had to do was control his nerve and play the game as it developed.

Floyd paused on the street outside the saloon to stare at a cloud of dust that was coming towards the town. He watched it for some moments before a coach materialized, and presently recognized Royston Talmadge's private vehicle approaching. He reached the front of the hotel as Frint appeared in the doorway.

'The big man is coming,' Floyd called, and Frint ran back inside the hotel. Floyd grinned, aware that Frint would be racing to warn Kerry that his father had arrived.

The yellow coach pulled in at the boardwalk and dust began to settle. The driver jumped down and opened a door. Royston Talmadge descended from the vehicle, larger than life and boisterous as usual. He was big in every sense, although his great height seemed diminished by his immense breadth and width. He had trouble negotiating the doorway of the coach, and his driver grasped him by an arm and tried to haul him out.

'Watch what you're doing, you idiot!' Royston yelled.

43

'Do you want to tear the sleeve off my damn coat? Get your hands off. I got into the coach under my own steam and I'll get out the same way. When I want your help I'll ask for it.'

The driver, Matt Gedge, released his hold and Royston came stumbling off the step of the coach. He would have sprawled on the sidewalk if Floyd had not stepped forward and grabbed him.

'What are you doing in town at this time of the morning, Floyd?' Royston demanded. He dusted down his black frock coat and adjusted his black stovepipe hat. 'Doesn't anyone do any work around here except me?'

'You know better than that, boss,' Floyd replied. 'I did a day's work at the mine before I came down here to see Kerry. He's waiting for me in the hotel. Did you have a good trip?'

'I'm here, aren't I? How are things at the Bonanza? Have you sorted that trouble?'

'I'm afraid not. It looks like the big vein is petering out as you thought it might the last time you were here. I'm getting only low grade ore now. I think we've had the best of it from Bonanza. I've opened new search tunnels in an attempt to pick up the vein again, but no dice. We are wasting our time. I think the vein was sluiced down the hill by a mountain stream that went underground and washed through the vein. I diverted the stream, but it was running down that course for maybe thousands of years before we reached it, and the gold is long gone. I've been waiting for your arrival so we can talk about what to do. Are you coming into the hotel for a drink?'

Royston Talmadge shook his head emphatically. 'You're

44

talking about having a drink when there is trouble in the mine!' He demanded. 'Is that what I'm paying you for? Anyway, the damn doc has warned me off whiskey and cigars.' Royston reached in to an inside pocket and produced a cigar case. He grinned as he bit the end off a cigar and struck a match. 'No overpaid pill pusher is gonna tell Royston P. Talmadge what to do. I might as well be dead if I can't drink and smoke. Life wouldn't be worth living. Why do the things a man likes best always turn out to be so bad for his health? Say, where is Kerry? Why ain't he here on the boardwalk to meet me? I've got a bone to pick with him. I told him to go to Chicago a month ago, and the next thing I heard, he was in Denver.

'That boy is the bane of my life. I don't know what I'm gonna do to keep him on the straight and narrow. Maybe if he stayed here and worked six months in the Bonanza it would straighten him out. I'd give a lot to have him behave like a normal young man. It's about time he settled down and acted his age. When I was twenty-five I was well on my way to my first million, and I didn't have a rich father standing by with a string of handouts.'

'Give him some breathing space,' Floyd suggested. 'He's your son, and I'm sure he'll come good in the end.'

'I sure hope he's a chip off the old block.' Royston paused and gave a bellow of a laugh. 'I reckon I would have done like Kerry. He met an actress in Chicago, so he said, and followed her to Denver.'

He turned and climbed back into the coach, aided by a shove behind by Matt Gedge, who caught Floyd's eye and winked as he climbed up to his driving seat. Royston lowered the coach window and stuck out his large head.

'I'll go up to the big house. Come and see me there when you have time. Tell Kerry I'll talk to him later, and say I was in a hellish mood when you saw me. That'll give him something to think about.'

The driver cracked his whip and the coach jerked forward. Royston fell back in his seat. Floyd turned to the hotel as Kerry Talmadge appeared in the doorway. Kerry was totally unlike his father. He was tall and slim; his face was pale and his dark eyes showed the effects of the drinking session of the previous night. He swayed on to the sidewalk, and Frint was on hand to steady him when he almost lost his balance. He was wearing a pale grey suit, rumpled as if he had slept in it, and his black string tie was loose at his throat. A wine stain marked the pure white of his shirt front, showing that he had missed his mouth on at least one occasion.

'Where the hell is the old man?' Kerry demanded. 'Couldn't he wait to see me? He's always in a damned hurry and he's never got any time for me.'

'We'll see him together later, Kerry. Why did you tie one on last night? You knew Royston was due in today, and you'd need to have all your wits about you when you faced him. There's a lot at stake here, and you've got to give it your best shot.'

'Don't take that tone with me, Floyd, or Frint will work you into a better frame of mind.' Kerry moistened his dry lips. 'For God's sake, Frint, get me a drink. How long have I got to stay in this godforsaken hellhole? I should never have left Denver.'

Frint turned obediently and hurried into the hotel.

'I've done all the spade work,' Floyd said patiently. 'I've

planted the general idea in Royston's mind and I think he'll agree with your suggestion when I show him the evidence I've arranged. He'll be more than ready to cut his losses, and you'll be able to step in and catch him cold.'

'I don't think he'll fall for it,' Kerry said. 'How many times do I have to tell you?'

'I know Royston better than you,' Floyd countered. 'You play it like I told you and he'll go for it. When he says to cut his losses, you tell him you think you can make a profit out of the mine despite what I've said, and he'll snap you up on that offer like a catfish rising to the bait. Then we'll be home and dried. I'll send Royston a set of production figures that will turn his attention to some other business – he's always fancied going into lumber – and he'll insist that you stick with Bonanza, just to teach you a lesson. He'll be certain the mine is played out while we will be hitting the new vein I discovered. Royston has pocketed more than five million dollars from the mine since it opened, and we can do the same over the next year. But the secret is in fooling Royston, and you've got to be as good as you can get, because despite your father's bluster, he's got one of the sharpest business minds I've ever come across, and you'll never amount to anything compared to him.'

'So why do we need that payroll you're planning to lift?' asked Kerry.

'Because Royston won't let you spend another red cent on Bonanza after he withdraws his interest, and it'll cost thousands to develop what we've got. Don't try to work it out, Kerry. You can take my word for it. And the payroll job went off smoothly days ago. The dough is here, in

Moundville, ready and waiting for us to get started. So pull yourself together for once and go for it.'

'So it is too late to call the whole thing off, huh?' Kerry shook his head. 'I was having second thoughts about killing soldiers.'

'You were having doubts at this late stage?' Floyd reached out and grasped Kerry by his shirtfront. 'You'd better get some backbone pretty damn quick. I told you the last time we met that you had to make a decision and stick by it, and you were all for it a month ago.'

Kerry nodded. 'OK. Lay off, will you? I ain't planning to quit now.'

Floyd thrust Kerry away so hard the back of the younger man's head slammed against the wall of the hotel. Kerry groaned and dropped to his knees just as Frint emerged from the hotel lobby with a glass of whiskey in his hand.

'Say, what is going on?' Frint called.

'You took too long getting that drink,' retorted Floyd. He grasped Kerry under the armpits and lifted him to his feet. 'Pour that whiskey into him and he'll be OK.' He shook Kerry. 'Are you OK?' he demanded.

'Sure,' Kerry replied, his chin on his chest. 'I need to get in out of this damned sun. Give me a hand, Frint.'

'Remember your part, Kerry, when you see Royston. 'I'll get back to you later.'

'You don't have to worry,' Kerry said faintly.

'But I do!' Floyd retorted, and his eyes turned bleak when he saw Kerry's fingers shake as he snatched the glass of whiskey from Frint and swallowed its contents in a single gulp.

Floyd studied Kerry's pale face. Beads of sweat were

showing on his forehead. Frint took Kerry's arm and led him back into the hotel. Floyd heaved a sigh and went along the sidewalk. His thoughts were harsh. He had never fully trusted Kerry, and figured to take out some insurance against Kerry's future behaviour. If Kerry failed to carry out his part in the steal as agreed then he would end up in one of the experimental bore holes in the mine with a couple of tons of rock on his chest. There was too much at stake now, and there could be no turning aside or going back from the original plan. Anyone failing to do what was expected of him would pay with his life.

Floyd considered the situation as his steps took him in the direction of the trail up to the mine but he paused on the back lots behind the bank and deliberated. Bodeen was in a highly nervous state, and Kerry Talmadge was a broken reed that should be removed from the set-up, but Kerry was essential to the next step to be taken, and had to be tolerated for the moment. Floyd turned his steps towards his house. The only man he felt he could trust was his brother, and he decided to draw Ward deeper into the plot to take over Bonanza.

Ward was seated in the living room when Floyd walked in on him.

'How are you doing?' Floyd inquired as Ward got to his feet.

'I'm about ready to climb up the walls,' Ward replied harshly. 'Sitting around like a sick old man ain't my idea of living it up like you promised me. I'm accustomed to a rigorous army life, and here I've been sitting around like an invalid for three days. It's getting to me, Floyd.'

'Have patience. You can get away from here shortly. But

I've got a couple of loose ends that might need tying up, and you're about the only man I can trust to handle them. So I'd like you to stick around for a few days longer than we planned, if that's all right with you. I'll make it worth your while.'

'Who do you want killed?' Ward demanded.

Floyd grinned. 'You're joking, but that's what I've got in mind. A couple of men are getting cold feet, and if they do decide to drop out then they'll have to go permanent. You could take care of them.'

'What's wrong with Rafe Cullen? He's a cold-blooded killer.'

'I trust you even more than I trust Rafe,' Floyd replied.

Ward shrugged. 'OK. But I'll hate every minute I'm stuck here.'

'I'll talk to you later. Give me until the end of the week, Ward. I'll know what might need to be done by then. I have to get moving. Royston Talmadge has just arrived, and he likes to have his employees running around in circles while he's here.'

Ward grimaced and settled down again. He reached for a whiskey bottle as Floyd departed. Ward was disappointed, for it seemed that he would never get away from Moundville. He got up and went to the window to scour the street for signs of soldier uniforms. . . .

FOUR

Hank Kenton watched Ward Price and Rafe Cullen fade into the darkness, with Joe Sarn leading the mule carrying the payroll. As soon as they had gone he took a lantern and went into the derelict mine. The ghastly smell of dead men assailed his nostrils and he slipped his neckerchief up over his nose and mouth. In the stark glare of lantern light he went to work on the huddle of dead soldiers, searching for anything of value. His shadow on the wall of the mine was grossly distorted by the guttering lantern. He had no respect for the dead and dragged them around callously to get at their pockets. By the time he had searched each cadaver he had amassed the sum of more than a hundred dollars, a gold pocket watch from Major Sterling and a gold ring which had come from the breast pocket of Trooper Biddle.

Hurrying out of the mine with the loot in his pockets, Kenton made camp several yards from the spot where the miners were camping. He made coffee, ate a frugal meal and then sat on his blanket and watched the coach slowly disintegrate and disappear into the mine. In a surprisingly short time there was no evidence left that a coach had arrived at this remote spot. He got up and went to confer with the miner running the operation.

'How is it going, Milligan?' Kenton demanded. 'Will you be done here by daybreak?'

'We'll be on our way back to Moundville in about two hours,' the miner replied. 'All we have to do now is take the horses into the mine and shoot them. Then I'll put a dynamite charge in the mine entrance and bring it down. When we've finished with it you won't know a mine ever existed here.'

'I've got to stick around for two or three days,' said Kenton. 'I'm gonna check out the area in daylight, and then wait to see if there is a search by the soldiers from the fort.'

Kenton went back to his blankets and turned in, only to be awakened later by an explosion. He went to check with Milligan and found the miner surveying the result of the charge he had laid.

'You certainly know your job, Milligan,' said Kenton admiringly. 'I'd never know a mine was here if I hadn't seen it.'

'Yeah,' the miner replied. 'All we've got to do now is gather some loose rocks and break up the shape of the tunnel mouth and we'll be done.'

Kenton watched as the finishing touches were applied to the job. When Milligan was satisfied, the half dozen miners retired to their camp, cleared away all evidence of their presence, and then departed into the greying dawn. Kenton stood alone in the heavy silence, looking around. He felt the sudden onset of loneliness as he went back to his blanket and slept until the sun showed above the eastern horizon.

The sun on his face awoke Kenton and he got up immediately and walked around the area looking for signs of human presence. He obliterated footprints in patches of dust and cleared away splinters of the coach until he was satisfied that all evidence had been removed. He stood for a long time looking at the spot where the old mine had been blocked in. Nothing remained – no unnatural outline to mark its presence – but he checked and rechecked the area until he was certain that all traces of what occurred there had been removed.

He paused for breakfast, and afterwards set out on foot to walk back along the route the coach had used to reach this remote spot, pausing here and there to wipe out a wheel mark or the print of a horseshoe. He covered a mile before he was satisfied with his chore, and then returned to his camp, planning to spend two days watching the area before heading off back to Moundville.

The sound of a mule braying alerted him as he neared the concealed mine and he drew his pistol and sneaked forward until he could see his camp and his picketed horse. His expression hardened when he saw an old man with a mule standing beside his blanket, and a curse ripped from his lips when the oldster began to search his saddle-bags. He walked forward silently, his gun levelled, and was within yards of the mule when it spotted him and brayed like a demon from hell. The man swung around, reaching for the butt of a pistol showing at his waist.

'Forget the gun,' Kenton rasped. 'Who in hell are you and what are you doing in my camp?'

'I'm asking you the same question,' the old timer countered. 'What's happened to my gold mine?'

'What gold mine!' Kenton demanded.

'The one belonging to me. I'm Tom Mitchell, and I registered a claim for this spot five years ago.' He jerked a hand in the direction of the concealed mine entrance. 'That's my mine, so where is the entrance? I have got better workings higher up from here, but I come back regularly to work old Betsy Marlin.'

'Betsy Marlin?' Kenton shook his head. 'I don't know what the hell you're talking about, Mitchell. You sound like you've got a touch of the sun.'

'I named this mine after my dead wife,' Mitchell's pale blue eyes glinted with passion. His clothes were ragged, as if he had worked and slept in them for months.

'I don't see a mine,' Kenton rasped. 'You're talking in riddles, mister. You must be loco!'

'Not now you don't see it because it's been filled in. Why did you do it?'

'I didn't do anything,' Kenton replied. 'I've been camped here for three days. My horse is lame and I'm waiting for its leg to heal. I'm on my way to Moundville, and it is too far to walk in this rough country.'

'You're lying, mister.' Mitchell spoke pugnaciously, and his hand eased toward the butt of the pistol in his waistband. 'I know the sound of a dynamite charge when I hear it, and I heard one going off before dawn. It woke me, and I came over right away. So now you can tell me what is going on. Why did you blow the mouth of my mine?'

Kenton gazed at the old man while he considered. He shook his head, aware that there was only one course open to him. His finger tightened on his trigger. Mitchell looked into Kenton's eyes, saw deadly intention in their depths and made a desperate play for his pistol. He managed to draw the weapon before Kenton triggered a shot. The crash of the flaming gun hurled a series of echoes out to the horizon. Mitchell dropped his gun, clutched at his chest, and then pitched lifeless to the ground.

The gun echoes died slowly, and Kenton remained motionless, looking at Mitchell's body until full silence returned. Then he heaved a sigh and holstered his gun. He looked around, saw a convenient niche in a wall of rock, and toted Mitchell over to it. He stuffed the body out of sight in the hole and began the task of piling loose rocks on the makeshift grave. He would take Mitchell's mule on to Moundville with him when he broke camp. By the time he had finished concealing the grave he had decided to leave immediately, and broke camp to ride out in the direction of Moundville. . . .

Captain Moran was ready to ride when the sun came up over the skyline in a blaze of red and gold glory. The patrol had been moving around while it was still dark in order to saddle and ride as soon as the sun showed. Moran entered the gully, leaving Lieutenant Carter to follow with the patrol. Moran rode slowly, his gaze intent on the hard ground and the walls of the dry wash. He saw no sign anywhere that a coach had passed that way, for the small stretches of dust revealed nothing significant. But Moran was well versed in tracking, and could tell that the ground had been brushed, probably with an army blanket.

He had not travelled more than a hundred yards when

he spotted a cigarette butt lying close to the wall of the gully, which had been missed by the trail blotter. Carter came up beside Moran, and uttered an ejaculation when he saw the evidence.

'That looks promising, Captain,' Carter observed.

'We shall see,' Moran replied tersely.

Moran shook his reins. The buckskin moved forward again. The heat from the sun increased as the patrol progressed through barren rocks that seemed to absorb the heat and then radiate it as an additional burden on their discomfort. A hundred yards on, and Lieutenant Carter spotted a wheel track showing in the dust.

'It looks like they got tired of blotting tracks,' said Carter. 'It should get easier now.'

'Remain alert,' Moran ordered.

By noon they were out of the gully and riding across a long stretch of level rock with a rock escarpment on their left. The signs that a coach had recently travelled ahead of them gradually become more numerous. They made a noon-time halt to rest the horses and eat a salt pork ration; they had covered several miles since dawn. Moran walked ahead for some distance. He gazed ahead in the general direction taken by his quarry, and his eyes took on a bleak expression when he spotted a number of buzzards circling lazily in the brassy sky. He hurried back to the escort for his horse, and when he explained what he had seen the patrol rode on eagerly, hoping to find answers to some of the questions that had been bothering them about the missing payroll.

Moran watched the flight of buzzards circling ceaselessly in the distance; a sure sign that something was dead or dying in this remote region. Moran knew that the birds of prey would not descend to feed until life in their prey had departed. An hour of steady riding, hoofs clattering over the rough ground, brought the patrol almost underneath the circling buzzards, and Moran produced his field glasses and studied the ground ahead, but could see nothing that would attract the birds. He gave an order for the patrol to ride on cautiously.

Moran stepped down from his saddle when he was directly beneath the buzzards. The soldiers dismounted and deployed to search the area, but found nothing significant. The bleak jumble of rocks looked as if they had been undisturbed for a thousand years. Moran stood by the blocked mouth of the mine, looking around but was unable to spot its presence.

Lieutenant Carter approached him, shaking his head.

'There is no sign of anything here, Captain,' Carter reported. 'What is attracting those buzzards?' His gaze dropped to the ground when he spotted something glinting in the sunlight. 'Say, what's this?' He bent and picked up a small metal object which he examined closely before holding it out on his open palm.

Moran stared at the small object, a shoulder badge of oak leaves – a major's insignia of rank.

'What is this doing out here?' Carter asked. 'Do you think Major Sterling dropped it deliberately, hoping it would be found by a search party?'

Moran took the badge, turned it over, and then shook his head. 'I'll keep it,' he said, and dropped it into an inside pocket of his jacket. 'Now let's try and work out what's attracting those buzzards. They are interested in something down here.'

'It's all solid rock around here,' Carter observed, 'except for this pile of rocks up against the bluff. Say, do you think something dead is hidden under here?'

'We shall have to find out,' Moran replied grimly. 'Get the men to remove the loose stuff and see what you come up with. As I see it, the payroll could not have been stolen without some of the escort being killed, and so far we've found no trace of them.'

Carter nodded and turned away, calling to the troopers. He issued orders. The men grimaced, disliking what they heard, but Carter put an edge to his tone and the soldiers set to work moving the rocks, hauling them away from the rock wall. Moran stood in the background, watching impassively.

It did not take long for the entrance to the mine to be revealed, and one of the soldiers turned away from his work and put a hand to his face.

'Get on with it, Reno,' Lieutenant Carter called. 'No slacking there!'

'There's a bad smell coming out of these rocks, sir,' Trooper Reno complained.

Carter went closer and sniffed the air. He turned away and reached for a handkerchief.

'What is it, Lieutenant?' demanded Moran.

'Whatever is buried under here is certainly dead,' Carter replied, 'and attracting the buzzards.'

'So get on with it,' Moran rapped. 'The smell won't hurt you. Clear away those rocks as quickly as you can.'

The men set to work again, most of them with their yellow neckerchiefs pulled up over their noses and mouths. Moran and Carter stood nearby, and exchanged glances as the entrance to the old mine gradually took shape. The smell of the dead increased, and the troopers worked faster, intent on finishing their unpleasant chore in the minimum of time. Some of the rocks slid down, revealing a dark cavity, and within minutes there was space enough for Lieutenant Carter to stick his head between two rocks and peer in.

When the lieutenant recoiled, he turned to Moran, his bronzed face ashen.

'There are dead soldiers inside, Captain,' he reported, 'and their horses, it looks like.'

The troopers continued feverishly and cleared away the remainder of the rocks. Daylight flooded into the mine entrance. Moran strode forward, picking a path through the odd rocks strewn across the solid floor of the mine. He halted abruptly when he saw a jumble of human bodies and horses, and what he recognized as pieces of a coach. He held his breath as he counted the number of dead men, and then turned away.

'The entire escort but one is in here,' he observed, stepping clear of the mine entrance to get a breath of fresh air. Sweat beaded his forehead as he gazed at Lieutenant Carter. 'Get the bodies out of there and check them. I want to know how they died and who is missing from the detail.'

The troopers removed eight bodies from the mine and placed them in a single line outside. Lieutenant Carter examined each upturned face before approaching Moran.

'There is one man missing, Captain,' he reported. 'The payroll escort consisted of six troopers and a sergeant, plus Major Sterling, and Corporal Ryker as the driver of the coach – nine men altogether, but there are only eight bodies here, and one extra uniform.'

'So who is missing?' Moran went to his horse and opened a saddle-bag to produce a list. Carter walked along the line of dead men, calling out their names, and Moran ticked them off his list. 'Trooper Price is missing,' he declared at length. 'So what has happened to him, and why is his uniform here?'

'Price joined the escort at the last moment, Captain, when Trooper Davis failed to turn up on parade,' Carter mused. 'Do you think that is significant?'

'I have no idea at the moment.' Moran shook his head. 'Send a man back to Fort Benton with a report of what we have found. We shall need a wagon out here to convey the bodies back for examination. Set some of the men to work bringing out the pieces of the coach. I don't expect to find the payroll, but look for it. I want everything here guarded until it can be transported back to Fort Benton for closer inspection. Tell the men to be careful – there may be clues to what happened. We don't have to look for the coach any longer, so I'll scout around and see what I can find in the way of tracks. Detail Trooper Davis to accompany me. We may be gone a considerable time.'

'Davis is busy right now, Captain,' Lieutenant Carter observed.

Moran looked around and saw Davis bent over one of the dead soldiers and searching the man's pockets.

'What are you doing, Davis?' Carter yelled.

Davis straightened. His face was ghastly. 'This is Biddle, Lieutenant,' he said harshly. 'I noticed that all these men's pocket have been turned out. I don't know what any of them was carrying, but I do know Biddle had a ring on him that he was going to give to his future wife when he got out of the army. It isn't on him now, sir. He's been robbed.'

'Are you sure about the ring, Davis?' asked Moran.

'Yes, sir. Biddle was always looking at it and talking about what he would do when he left the army. That ring was on him for weeks, but now it's missing. Biddle wouldn't have left it behind at the fort, sir.'

A search of the other bodies revealed that all pockets were empty. Moran went to his horse and swung into the saddle. He waited for Davis to join him and then set out, checking the ground as he rode. He found boot prints at the spot where Kenton had made his camp, and saw dried blood on hard rock. He dismounted and subjected the area to a close scrutiny. Davis found a .45 cartridge case and Moran pocketed it. But they missed the old prospector's last resting place and saw hoof prints in a stretch of dust that showed that several animals had departed in the direction of Moundville.

Moran consulted his map. 'I make it about twenty-five miles to Moundville,' he mused, 'and the next nearest town is Dogtown, which is seventy miles from here. We'll push on to Moundville, Davis, and check for tracks as we ride.'

They rode on through a vast desolation of rocky slopes and towering peaks, dwarfed by their surroundings as they toiled over the rough ground. They had to cast around for sign many times, but Moran assumed that his unknown quarry was heading for Moundville and, searching in that direction, each time they found what they were looking for – a tenuous link of a print here and a track there which led on to the distant mining town.

Daylight was fading when Moran reached a high crest and saw Moundville spread out before him in a valley. He reined in to study the aspect. Moundville was merely a huddle of small houses scattered untidily in a low area between two peaks. Several larger buildings – a store, two saloons, a hotel and a bank – formed a close-knit community set apart from the living quarters of the miners. Moran let his gaze lift to the opposite high ground. He saw a house situated alone above and beyond the business area of the town, and a hundred feet above that there was an even larger house. Higher up still were the assorted buildings of the gold mine, which had initially attracted the community into this raw wilderness.

'I know Moundville well, Captain,' said Davis in a low tone. 'I came here several times with Biddle when we were off duty. It's a one-mine town, sir. That is the Big Bonanza mine across the valley. It's owned by a man called Royston Talmadge.'

'Is the town popular with the men of Fort Benson?' Moran queried.

'It makes a change from the army post, Captain. There is a regular patrol to Moundville once a month that camps outside the town for a couple of days before returning to the fort. I think it's done mainly to give the troopers a chance of seeing civilization for a spell. There's a nice hotel, sir, and a couple of saloons.'

'We'll ride in.' Moran glanced around. The sun was disappearing beyond the western skyline in a blaze of heavenly fire. 'It'll be dark soon, and too late to do any-thing tonight, so you can do your own thing until tomorrow morning at eight o'clock. I'll take a room at the hotel and you can meet me there.'

'Yes, sir. I'll put up at the general store, Captain. That's where Biddle's girl lives. Her father owns the Mercantile. Can I tell her about Biddle, Captain?'

Moran considered for a moment and then shook his head. 'I think we'd better keep what we know under our hats for the time being,' he mused. 'If the killers are here in Moundville then we don't want to give them warning that their secret is out.'

'OK, sir. I'll let it be known that I'm off duty for a few days.'

'And keep your eyes open for any sign of Trooper Price,' Moran said. 'I want to know why we didn't find him dead with the rest of the escort.'

'Do you think he is mixed up in the robbery, Captain?'

'It is too early to say.' Moran shook his head. 'I'll keep my suspicions to myself until we discover what happened. There is one thing I want you to keep in mind, Davis: I'm working undercover on this case so don't call me captain or sir when we talk in town. I have cover arranged as a salesman for a mining manufacturer back east. I use a number of aliases in my work.'

'OK, sir.' Davis nodded.

They rode down a long slope into the one main street. Lamplight was showing in the windows of many of the houses. Moran dismounted outside the hotel, removed his saddle-bags and rifle from the horse and handed his reins to Davis.

'Take care of the horse and then you are free for the night, Davis,' Moran instructed. 'I'll register here under my own name, in case you need to talk to me before morning. But you could prove to be an embarrassment in your uniform. I don't want it assumed that I am connected with the army.'

'I'll play it low key, Captain.' Davis took the reins of Moran's horse and rode away along the street to the livery barn.

Moran entered the hotel and took a room on the second floor. He sat down on the bed to consider what he had learned about the missing payroll and the dead soldiers. Accustomed as he was to the brutality that existed within the army, where generally life had no value, his mind was throbbing with shock at what had been discovered within the derelict mine. He assumed that somewhere in this mining community were the men responsible for the cold-blooded robbery, and he was dedicated to exposing them and bringing them to justice.

FIVE

Trooper Davis led Captain Moran's horse into the livery stable. He watered and fed the animals and then spent an hour working on them before considering his own comfort. The liveryman, Silas Green, appeared just before Davis finished tending the animals, and greeted him warmly, having met Davis on several occasions when he had ridden into town with Trooper Biddle.

'Where's your friend Biddle?' Green asked. 'I was talking to Dora Harmon about him only this morning. She said he's due out of the army in a couple of months and they are gonna get married. She reckons he's planning to help Sarn Harmon run the general store. Old Sarn could do with an extra pair of hands. He can't get around these days like he used to.'

Davis felt as if a clammy hand clutched his heart as the liveryman's words produced an image of Biddle stretched out dead in the derelict mine. He drew a deep breath and forced a grin.

'He's got duty at the fort, but he'll be here in time for his wedding. I have a week off duty so I've come to see if

Dora needs any help with her wedding plans.'

'You brought in two horses,' Green observed.

'The buckskin belongs to a man I met on the trail. He's a salesman for a mining manufacturer back east, so he said. He'll be along in the morning to pay you for stabling his horse. He's putting up at the hotel while he's in town.'

'That'll be OK.' Green turned away.

'Are there any other soldiers in town right now?' Davis asked. 'I was due to leave Fort Benson with a trooper named Ward Price, but I got delayed at the last minute and he rode on ahead. We planned to have a high old time around here.'

'You're the first soldier I've seen in weeks,' Green replied. 'They ain't showing up like they used to. Must be another attraction someplace else, huh?'

'I reckon so.' Davis brushed himself down and prepared to leave. 'I need a drink, and then some grub. See you around, huh?'

'Sure thing. Enjoy yourself. You troopers deserve all the pleasure you can get. It's a tough life, huh?'

Davis left the stable and went into the nearest saloon. Silas Green walked along the street to the law office, where Henry Snaith, a deputy county sheriff, was seated at his desk. Snaith was a tall, thin man in his late forties. His face was angular, cheeks concave, nose long and thin and his dark eyes were deep-set; seemingly lifeless.

'Howdy, Snaith?' Green greeted. 'You asked me to let you know if any soldiers turned up from Fort Benson, and one just rode in – Trooper Davis. I know him. He's a regular visitor. He's been around several times with another trooper named Biddle who is planning to marry

Dora Harmon in a couple of months.'

'I have seen them around,' Snaith drawled. 'Thanks for letting me know, Silas. Is Biddle with Davis?'

'No. Davis was putting two horses in the stable when I saw him, and he said one animal belonged to a mining salesman he met on the trail.' Green paused. 'What for do you want to know about soldiers? They are pretty quiet and orderly in town. I've never known any of them cause trouble.'

'I like to know who is around at any given time,' Snaith replied. 'That way I can smell trouble usually before it starts.'

'Are you expecting trouble from soldiers?' Green persisted.

'No. But you can't beat being ready for anything.'

'Davis mentioned another soldier who was due to ride in with him, so there should be a second trooper around, name of Price – Ward Price, I think he said. Ain't there a feller called Price running the Big Bonanza? Could this Trooper Price be related to him?'

'Floyd Price manages Bonanza.' Snaith shook his head. 'I know him pretty well but I've never heard him talk about a brother serving with the military around here.'

Green nodded and departed. Snaith got off his seat and hitched up his gunbelt. He locked the office and walked along the street to the hotel. The lobby was deserted; most of the guests were in the dining room for their main meal of the day. Snaith looked in the hotel register and saw the name Slade Moran, mining salesman, entered in Room 12 on the second floor. He moved to the doorway of the bar and peered inside. Rafe Cullen was seated at a small table, flanked as usual by Kenton and Sarn, and Snaith motioned for Cullen to join him before going back outside into the shadows surrounding the hotel. Moments later, Cullen turned up at his shoulder.

'What's wrong, Snaith?' Cullen asked.

'You asked me to let you know if any soldiers showed up in town,' said Snaith. 'Well, one rode in a short time ago. He'll be in a saloon or the eating house right now. He showed up with a mining salesman, who has booked into the hotel. The trooper's name is Davis, and he told Silas Green another trooper, called Ward Price, rode in ahead of him, so there'll be two soldiers in town now.'

Cullen frowned at the mention of Ward Price for he knew Ward was concealed in Floyd's house, and had been for several days.

'Thanks, Snaith.' Cullen patted the deputy's shoulder. 'Let me know if any more soldiers turn up, huh?'

'Sure. There ain't gonna be any trouble, is there? I run a clean town here, and we don't want any trouble.'

'No trouble,' replied Cullen. 'You can pick up a bottle of whiskey from Harmon's store tomorrow for your pains. I'll pass on the word tonight.'

'Thanks.' Snaith went back to his office, highly satisfied.

Cullen went back into the hotel bar and dropped into his seat. Kenton looked at him inquiringly.

'Something wrong, Rafe?' he demanded.

'There could be.' Cullen nodded and explained. 'We'd better pick up this Trooper Davis. I wanta know why he said Ward Price rode into town just ahead of him when Ward has been here three days. Come on, let's grab him and hear what he's got to say.'

Cullen led the way along the street to check out the saloons. When he looked over the batwings of Fargo's bar the first thing he saw was a blue uniform with yellow cavalry facings. Davis was standing at the bar with a glass of beer in his hand.

'No rough stuff in here,' Cullen warned Kenton and Sarn. 'We'll take him somewhere quiet where I can talk to him. Be ready to back up my play, huh?'

Cullen shouldered through the batwings and walked to the bar to stand beside Davis. There were a dozen townsmen in the saloon. Kenton ranged up to the bar on the other side of Davis, and Sarn remained in the background. Davis sensed that he was being crowded and glanced up at Cullen.

'Give me elbow room,' Davis rapped.

'Are you trying to pick a fight with me?' Cullen replied. 'I came in for a quiet drink with my friends.'

Davis glanced at Kenton. The big man's right shoulder was pressing against Davis's left arm. Kenton grinned, but his face was expressionless and there was a hard glint in his pale eyes.

Davis picked up his beer, stepped back a step to get clear of Cullen and Kenton, and trod on Sarn's left foot. Sarn grinned but did not speak. Davis caught his breath as realization came to him. He eased to his left as Kenton moved backward, recoiled off Kenton's shoulder, and the beer in his glass splashed over Cullen.

Cullen reached out, took the glass from Davis's hand and set it down on the bar. He wiped splashes of beer from his face.

'I'm sorry!' said Davis.

'Sorry don't get it done,' Cullen replied. 'Come with us and we'll talk about it.'

'I'm not going anywhere,' Davis said sharply. 'If you've got robbery on your mind then forget it. I don't have more than two red cents to rub together.'

'You mentioned Trooper Ward Price to a friend of mine earlier,' Cullen said, 'and I happen to know he's been in Moundville three days at least; so how come you reckoned he left Fort Benson just before you did?'

'Price is here in town?' Davis shook his head. 'Then he can't be the Trooper Price I know. You must be talking about someone else.'

'I can take you to him right this minute,' Cullen insisted. 'Come on. We can soon settle this.'

Cullen grasped Davis by the arm and led him toward the door. Davis went willingly, for if Ward Price was in town he certainly wanted to see him. There were a number of questions niggling in Davis's mind which only Ward Price could answer. They left the saloon and Cullen led the way past the front of the hotel to an alley which gave access to a path ascending the hill to Floyd Price's house. As they passed the hotel, Moran emerged to stand on the board-walk, smoking a cigarette. He spotted Davis's uniform – its yellow facings showed up plainly in the shadows.

Moran ran his eye over the three men with Davis, and he became alert. Davis was hemmed in, and one of the men had hold of the trooper's arm. Moran dropped a hand to his pistol and threw away his cigarette. He followed through the shadows, and when the quartet reached the dark alley, Moran saw Davis hang back.

'Where are you taking me?' Davis demanded.

'Quit worrying,' Cullen replied. 'If you wanta see Ward Price then come along.'

Moran stiffened at the mention of Price. He pressed closer to the four men, and saw Kenton draw his pistol and thrust the muzzle against Davis's spine.

'Keep moving,' Kenton rasped.

Cullen took Davis's Army Colt from its holster and stuck it into his waistband. He kept hold of Davis's arm as they ascended the path to the mine manager's house. Moran followed intently, and drew his pistol when he saw Cullen disarm Davis. He saw Davis try to hold back but Cullen tightened his grip and forced him along. The four men reached the front door of the house. Moran slipped into dense shadows close by as Cullen rapped sharply. The door was opened by Ward Price. Lamplight flooded the doorway, and Davis gaped in shock at the sight of the only soldier of the payroll escort that had not been murdered and dumped in the derelict mine.

'Price, what in hell are you doing here?' Davis demanded. 'Why aren't you with the payroll escort?'

'Davis!' Ward fell back a pace in surprise. 'Where did you come from?'

'We picked him up in Drake's saloon because he told someone you left Fort Benson just before he did,' Cullen said. 'We know he's lying, and we need to know why.'

'You knew I took your place on the payroll escort, Davis,' Ward said. 'So why did you say I left the fort ahead of you? What are you covering up?'

'The payroll and the escort have gone missing,' Davis countered, 'so how is it you are here and out of uniform?'

Ward glanced angrily at Cullen, who smiled as if he was

enjoying the confrontation.

Moran listened to the exchange with interest. It looked as if Davis had located the one soldier missing from the payroll escort. He moved closer to the open door, staying in the shadows and gripping the butt of his pistol in readiness for action.

'Why did you bring him here, Cullen?' Ward demanded.

'We need to know what's going on,' Cullen replied. 'And something is developing, according to what Davis has said.'

'You'd better get rid of him now he's seen me.' Ward spoke uneasily. 'Floyd won't be happy about this. No one is supposed to know I'm here, especially a soldier from Fort Benson.'

'We'll take care of him shortly.' Cullen pushed Davis forward over the doorstep and into the house. 'Keep him covered, Kenton, in case he tries anything. We need to find out what he knows. He said something about the payroll and escort being missing. What is the latest on that, Davis?'

'The detail didn't arrive at Colorado Springs on schedule and has been posted as missing. That's all I know.' Davis kept his voice under strict control and his face expressionless. 'Patrols are out looking for the coach.'

'They won't find anything in a hundred years!' Cullen laughed. 'Who is the man you rode into town with, Davis? Was it another soldier?'

'No. He's a salesman for a mining equipment manufacturer back east, so he said.'

'We can easily check up on him,' Cullen nodded. 'What

is his name?'

'Slade Moran,' Davis shrugged. 'That's all I know about him.'

'Where is Floyd?' Cullen asked Ward. 'I want to talk to him about this.'

'He's gone up to the big house to see Royston Talmadge and he won't be back until later. You'd better take Davis out of here and keep him somewhere safe until Floyd can be told about him.'

'We could stick him in the jail,' Cullen mused, 'but I don't know how far we can trust Snaith. He is slowly coming round to our way of thinking but he ain't ready to go whole hog yet. I don't want to be seen dragging Davis around town, so take him into one of the back rooms here, Kenton, and tie him up. Then stay with him, and keep him quiet. I'll go and check on Slade Moran at the hotel.'

Kenton nodded and waggled his gun. 'Get moving, soldier boy, and don't try anything. Sarn, get some rope and bring it along.'

Cullen grinned at the unhappy expression showing on Davis's face and turned away. Moran eased back into deeper shadow and watched Cullen returning to the main street. Davis was ushered into the house and the door closed. Moran waited, his thoughts racing. Ward Price, the man missing from the payroll detail, was here in Moundville, out of uniform, and apparently ready to dispose of Davis.

Moran waited a couple of minutes, and then approached the door of the house. He tried to open it but found it was locked. He held his gun ready as he knocked on the door, which was jerked open a moment later, and Ward Price appeared.

'What is it now, Cullen?' Price demanded, and then fell silent, for Moran thrust his gun hand forward and pointed the muzzle of his pistol at Price's heart.

'Don't make a sound, Price,' Moran warned. 'Get your hands up.' He pushed Price back off the doorstep, followed him into the house and closed the door with his heel.

Price's face expressed shock. He turned pale as he raised his hands and stood gazing at Moran in disbelief.

'Where are they holding Davis?' Moran demanded. 'Take me to him now.'

'Who are you?' Price demanded, 'and what are you talking about?'

'You are Trooper Ward Price of B Troop, Fort Benson,' said Moran. 'You were detailed to ride with the escort guarding the payroll which has gone missing. I'll be talking to you about that shortly, but right now I want Trooper Davis released from the two men holding him. Don't lie about the situation because I followed Davis and three men up here from the front of the hotel, and heard a great deal of what was said. So take me to Davis.'

'You must have heard wrong, because there is no one here,' said Price. 'You can look over the house if you wish.'

'Get moving,' Moran said bleakly. 'We'll check the ground floor rooms first. Don't try to warn those men. If there is any shooting, then you will be the first to collect a slug.'

'Who are you?' Price repeated. 'Are you a lawman?'

'There are some who would say I am not,' Moran

74

replied. 'Now cut the gab and get moving.'

Price turned away and walked to a flight of stairs. He mounted two of the stairs and then turned to face Moran.

'You're wasting your time,' Price said, and kicked at Moran's levelled pistol with his right foot.

Moran, ready for resistance, pulled his gun out of line so that Price's foot failed to make contact, and then reached out with his left hand and caught hold of Price's heel as it reached the top of its kick. He thrust upward, forcing Price's foot up higher than intended. Price yelled as he lost his balance and crashed down on the bottom stair. Before he could recover, Moran slammed the muzzle of his pistol against the side of Price's head. Price yelped in pain. Moran struck again, and Price slid off the stair and slumped on the floor.

'What's going on, Price?' a man's voice called from the rear of the house.

Moran turned in that direction and walked forward. Sarn appeared in a doorway. He paused at the sight of Moran and, when he saw Moran's levelled gun, turned and dived back into the room, yelling a warning to whoever was inside. Moran ran forward and lunged into the room. Sarn had turned as soon as he entered, and was now drawing a pistol. Moran fired instantly. Sarn staggered. The bullet struck the smaller man somewhere in the body but he did not fall. Sarn's gun seemed to grow too heavy to be held in one hand and he used his left hand to steady it. Moran fired again and Sarn twisted and fell to the floor.

Davis was seated on a chair with Kenton standing over him. Kenton was using a short length of rope to bind Davis, and the disturbance had shocked him badly enough to forestall a reaction from him. He stared in horror at Sarn's motionless figure, and made no attempt to reach for the butt of his holstered gun.

'Get your hands up,' Moran called. He waited for Kenton to comply and then went forward to snatch a pistol out of his holster. 'Now untie Davis,' Moran said.

Kenton did so reluctantly.

'I'm sure glad to see you,' Davis said as he got to his feet. 'You won't believe half of what's happened since I got into town.'

'I heard some of it,' Moran said. He handed Kenton's gun to Davis. 'Cover him. I've got the man they called Price stretched out near the stairs. Is he the missing trooper?'

'It's him right enough, sir. I'll go and hogtie him with this rope, shall I?'

'Do that,' Moran agreed, 'and then we'll take this guy and Price to the law office and put them behind bars. I need to interrogate Price as soon as possible. Let's get moving, Davis. This is a breakthrough and we have to take advantage of it.'

SIX

Floyd Price had left the Big Bonanza mine before sundown and walked down to the hotel with the intention of giving Kerry Talmadge a final briefing before they confronted Royston Talmadge. Before leaving his office, Floyd spoke with Hal Dano, and his assistant warned him again not to trust Kerry. With his mind brimming with doubt, Floyd turned into the hotel to find Cass Frint standing by the reception desk. Frint grimaced when he saw Floyd, straightened, and came toward him.

'You'll have to face Royston alone this evening,' Frint greeted. 'Kerry is real sick. Must have been something he ate. No way is he gonna be able to make it tonight.'

Floyd scowled. 'More likely it was something he drank,' he observed. 'OK. I'll talk some to Royston, and leak to him a little of what Kerry was supposed to tell him. If I can get a deal without Kerry having to talk to his old man about it then so much the better. Perhaps you can arrange for Kerry to be sick more often. I reckon I could manage all right without his help. I'll see him tomorrow.'

'That is if he is feeling better tomorrow,' Frint countered.

Floyd frowned as he left the hotel. He walked back up the hill to Royston Talmadge's big house, wondering if Kerry was ill or merely feigning because he was getting cold feet. He steeled himself for what he was about to do and ran through the salient points of what he hoped to achieve. By the time he knocked at the door of the mine owner's big house he had everything straight, and was eager to begin.

Royston Talmadge answered the door. He was wearing a blue silk dressing gown over his clothes. A half-filled glass of whiskey was clutched in his left hand and he had a cigar clamped between the first two fingers of his right hand.

'So here you are!' Royston boomed. 'And what time do you call this? I've been drinking myself stupid for hours, waiting for you to show up. I sincerely hope it was good honest toil that kept you too busy to report to me. If I'm working you too hard, Floyd, and if you can't handle the job, then I can hire someone who can fill your boots better than you.'

'It's hard enough, Royston,' Floyd replied, ignoring the mine owner's jibe. He was well accustomed to Royston's personal sallies, and hardly noticed them these days. 'I've been down to the hotel to collect Kerry, but it seems he's sick.'

'Is that so?' Royston stepped out of the doorway, stuck his cigar in his mouth and grasped Floyd's right arm to pull him into the house. He closed the door and led the way to his study. 'So let's get down to business, shall we? I suspect that you've got nothing but doom and gloom to tell me. Help yourself to a drink.'

Floyd poured himself a whiskey and sat down in front of the desk. Royston dropped into his big padded seat and gulped down the contents of his glass.

'It's strange about Kerry turning up ill this evening,' Royston mused. 'Did you see him at the hotel?'

'No. Frint was waiting at the reception desk when I got there. He told me about Kerry.'

'There was nothing wrong with Kerry when I saw him this afternoon.' Royston puffed on his cigar. 'What's going on between you two? I thought you were the best of friends.'

'Kerry was here this afternoon?' Floyd was staggered by the revelation and struggled to remain expressionless. He knew Royston well enough not to make any comment. There was a look on the mine owner's face that hinted at more surprises to come, and Floyd could only hope that Kerry had not gone off half-cocked and ruined the whole business.

'Tell me about the mine.' Royston poured himself another drink. 'Do you think Big Bonanza is on its last legs?'

'You said that yourself a couple of months ago.' Floyd emptied his glass and reached for the bottle to replenish it.

'It doesn't matter what I said two months ago. I want to know what you think. You're the man in charge, and you should have all the facts and figures at your fingertips. What the hell am I paying you for?'

'I've written you at great length detailing what I have done to bring the mine back to full production. The main vein has tapered from three feet to twelve inches, as we expected, and the high grade ore is petering out. What we are getting now is the end of a good vein. We encountered an underground stream, like I told you. I diverted it, but the water either washed the vein deeper or caused a rift which could have diverted it laterally. We are looking for a resumption of the vein beyond the break, but it will cost a helluva lot of dough to continue, and we could easily come up empty-handed. That's it in a nutshell, and I'm giving it to you straight. If we go on much longer at this present rate you'll be working at a loss, and I know how you hate throwing away good money. You would prefer to cut your losses at the earliest, so I'm of the opinion that you should get out now.'

Royston nodded. 'I'm thinking along the same line as you, Floyd, and I'm already looking elsewhere for business. I made this trip with the firm intention of telling you to close down the whole operation, but Kerry came here this afternoon, with an idea I can't ignore.'

Floyd stiffened in his seat. Damn Kerry if he had opened his big mouth and queered the whole pitch! 'Really?' he said. 'If Kerry came up with a good business idea then it would be a first for him.'

'Don't be too hard on my son,' Royston snapped. 'He is a chip off the old block, and he could make good at that. What I like about his idea is that he's finally taking an interest in my business and is prepared to do some hard work to prove a point. I've been hoping for years that he would knuckle down and try to earn some real dough instead of trying to spend every red cent I earn. So I've decided to give the boy his head and let him take over Big Bonanza and try to pull it round. He won't get any extra money to support his efforts, and I'd like to see what kind of a job he makes of the business, even if he fails. I was surprised by his offer, but I want him to go ahead.'

Floyd frowned, unable to believe his ears. 'Kerry came to you with that idea?' he demanded.

'You might well sound surprised.' Royston laughed. 'You didn't think he had it in him, did you? I know I certainly didn't. But I want you to stay put in your job and steer him right. Will you do that for me? Don't worry if Kerry fails because it will be no reflection on you, and there will be another job waiting for you after this. What do you say?'

Floyd drew a deep breath. What was Kerry up to? He had tackled Royston with the very plan they had worked out over the past weeks, and Royston had gone for it like a catfish rising for air. But Floyd doubted that he could trust Kerry, and wondered what the weak-kneed son of a bitch was trying to pull. They had been due to confront Royston this evening with the scheme, but Kerry had jumped the gun, succeeded with his pitch, and was now hiding away like a greedy dog with a juicy bone.

'I'll stay on as long as you think I should.' Floyd was trying to get his mind back to working normally. 'But don't expect the operation to run smoothly. Kerry is wilful, and I suspect he will want to do things his way. He's only got one point of view – his own – and that could lead to a lot of trouble.'

'I don't think so.' Royston puffed on his cigar. 'The whole point of this exercise is to let Kerry have his head and do his own thing. All you have to do is go along with him, advise him where you can and report his progress to me. I shall want a complete picture of the operation. Is that clear?'

Floyd nodded. 'I get the message,' he said, wondering how he could adapt this situation to his advantage. If Kerry was planning a double-cross then he had a whole lot more to learn about the business. 'When is this changeover to take place?' he queried. 'We need to have a good cover story for the miners. If they get a whiff of the mine being in trouble they'll make a run for other parts and other jobs. Moundville will be a ghost town in a matter of days.'

'I estimate Kerry will cut his work force by fifty percent while he is trying to bring the mine back into full production.' Royston sat back in his seat and regarded Floyd with an impassive stare, but there was a glint in his hard gaze which Floyd did not miss.

'I don't trust you, Royston,' Floyd said. 'I suspect you have got something unpleasant up your sleeve. I wouldn't ever risk sitting down in a game of poker with you. But if you look after my interests and remember that I'll be trying to help Kerry find his feet then I'll take a chance and go along with your wishes.'

'Then there is nothing more to be said.' Royston stubbed out his cigar and refilled his whiskey glass. 'Let us drink to Kerry's success. If he proves that he can work a miracle then he'll do for me.'

Floyd raised his glass mechanically, but his mind was back in gear and he was beginning to scheme how he could turn this situation to his own advantage. He thought about the stolen payroll lying in Bodeen's bank and wondered if murdering the soldiers had been necessary. But there could be no going back, and if Kerry tried to break his word about their plan then the penalty for his deception would be death.

'I shall be leaving in the morning.' Royston got to his feet and Floyd rose immediately. 'You're still working for me, Floyd, and I shall expect the usual high standard of work from you in future. Stand by Kerry and see if he can pull Bonanza around. If you succeed I shall be eternally generous.'

Floyd left the big house with his head in a whirl of speculation. What had transpired was exactly what he had been after since the scheme to steal the mine from Royston had come to him. He should have been wild with joy, but he had a bad feeling about Kerry which would not leave him. Kerry was planning some trickery, and Floyd knew he had to be two jumps ahead of the wilful youngster if he meant to show a profit from all of this. At least he had a hole card in this merciless game – the stolen payroll lying in Bodeen's bank. If the worst happened and his partners in crime pulled out leaving him high and dry then he could always skip with the money. He went homeward in a thoughtful frame of mind, trying to reach a decision about the immediate future, and came to the conclusion that further progress was not in his hands. He would have to wait until others made their intentions clear. . . .

Moran bent over the man he had shot and checked him. Sarn was dead. The .45 slug had struck him to the left of centre in his chest and passed between two ribs before ploughing through his heart and coming to rest against his spine. But Sarn hadn't felt a thing; he was dead before he hit the floor. Moran turned to confront the silent Kenton.

'Turn around,' he ordered, and Kenton obeyed without hesitation. 'Get your hands up above your head and don't give me any trouble or I'll stretch you out beside your friend.'

Kenton remained motionless. Moran searched him for weapons, using his left hand; the muzzle of his pistol pressed against Kenton's spine. He removed a long-bladed knife from a sheath attached to Kenton's belt and then checked for further weapons. When he was satisfied that Kenton was now unarmed he ordered him to lower his hands.

'How are you doing, Davis?' Moran called.

'Just about through, Captain,' Davis replied. 'Price is coming back to his senses now.'

Moran motioned with his gun and Kenton left the room. Moran followed and saw Davis binding Price, who was sitting on the bottom stair, shaking his head. His eyes were closed. Moran motioned to Davis to cover Kenton and the trooper drew his gun and cocked it. Moran stood over Price, gun in hand. He shook Price by the shoulder. Price's eyes flickered open and he gazed up at Moran, his awareness returning slowly. He lowered his gaze, but not before Moran saw stark fear strike as Price realized the hopelessness of his position.

'What is your name?' Moran asked.

Price glanced at the impassive Davis and shrugged. 'I can't deny it,' he said in a low voice. 'I'm Ward Price.'

'I am Provost Captain Slade Moran, and I'm arresting you on suspicion of being involved in the disappearance of the missing army payroll and its escort. What have you to say?'

'Nothing.' Price shook his head.

Moran turned his attention to Kenton. 'Give me your name and explain why you brought Trooper Davis to this house?'

Kenton shook his head and remained silent. Moran nodded.

'We'll take them to jail and hold them for further questioning,' he said to Davis. 'And I want to pick up the third man before he becomes aware of what has happened here.'

'They said they were going to kill me, Captain,' said Davis.

'We'll get to the bottom of it,' replied Moran. 'Let's get moving.'

Kenton and Price were escorted from the house and taken down the hill to the main street. Deputy Sheriff Snaith was seated at his desk when they entered the law office, and he got to his feet at the sight of Moran's drawn gun.

'What gives?' Snaith demanded.

Moran gave his identity and explained what had occurred. 'I want these two held in your jail.' He glanced at Kenton. 'Can you identify this man?'

'Sure,' said Snaith. 'He's Hank Kenton – works for Big Bonanza as a troubleshooter. Sarn and Cullen are the other two troubleshooters on the mine payroll. What have you been up to, Kenton?'

'Describe the other two,' Moran said.

'Rafe Cullen is tall and thin. He runs things. Sarn is a little guy.' Snaith picked up a bunch of keys lying on a corner of his desk. 'Bring them through here.' He opened a door in the back wall of the office and started to lead the way into the cell block when Moran stopped him.

'Aren't you going to search your prisoners before you jail them?' Moran demanded.

'OK.' Snaith grimaced. 'Turn out your pockets on the desk.'

Moran watched intently as both men complied. When they had finished, Moran glanced at the alert Davis.

'Check them out, Trooper,' he ordered. 'Make sure their pockets are empty.'

Davis obeyed eagerly. He searched Price and found a small knife in the back pocket of his pants. Price grimaced.

'I didn't know it was in there,' he said. 'These pants belong to my brother.'

Davis turned to Kenton and searched him meticulously. He found nothing until he felt in the inside pocket of the coat Kenton was wearing and produced a ring. He held it up, turned to place it on the desk and then looked at the ring more closely. He studied the diamond set in the gold band and then examined the inside of the ring.

'Where did you get this ring?' Davis demanded, turning to Kenton.

'What's wrong, Davis?' asked Moran.

'This ring belonged to Trooper Biddle, sir.' Davis's face had turned pale and he spoke through clenched teeth.

Moran stepped forward and took the ring. He studied it before looking at Davis.

'Are you sure the ring belonged to Biddle?'

'Certain sure, Captain. I've seen it many times. And there are initials inside, RB and DH – Ray Biddle and Dora

Harmon. I was with Biddle when he had the ring engraved.'

Moran turned to the sullen Kenton. 'How did you come by the ring?' he asked.

Kenton moistened his lips with the tip of his tongue. His expression changed, and for a tense moment he looked like a cornered rat. Then he grinned. 'I found it,' he said quickly; 'picked it up outside the general store last week.'

Davis lunged forward and swung a right hand punch which connected with Kenton's jaw. The bigger man fell to the floor as if he had been poleaxed.

'Davis,' Moran rasped. 'Control yourself. Remember you are on duty.'

'He's lying, sir,' Davis replied. 'Biddle never let that ring out of his possession.'

Snaith bent over Kenton and helped him to his feet. Kenton shook his head to rid himself of the effects of the blow.

'If it was bought for the Harmon gal then she probably lost it last week,' Kenton said.

'Biddle planned to give the ring to Dora on the day he got out of the army,' said Davis. 'She hasn't even seen it yet. It was to be a big surprise for her, and was in Biddle's pocket when he left the fort on escort duty.'

'Well, Kenton?' asked Moran. 'Do you want to change your story in view of Davis's evidence?'

'I've got nothing more to say,' Kenton replied.

Moran motioned to the watchful Snaith. 'Lock them up. I'll get back to them later for more questioning. There are further arrests to be made, and we left a dead man in the house up the hill. From the description you gave me I think it must be Sarn. A third man came down to the hotel to check on me, and I guess he must be Cullen. I'd like to pick him up before he becomes aware of this situation.'

'I'll accompany you,' said Snaith.

Moran nodded. 'Davis, stay here. We'll be back shortly.'

Snaith led the way along the street to the hotel. Moran was content to allow the deputy to do his job. They found Cullen standing at the small bar in the hotel with a glass of beer in his left hand. Snaith drew his pistol as he confronted the troubleshooter and Moran moved to the right to cover Cullen from an angle.

'Get 'em up, Cullen,' said Snaith. 'You're under arrest.'

Cullen turned quickly, like a big cat. He showed his teeth in a mirthless grin as he threw his beer into Snaith's face and reached for his holstered gun in a fast right-hand draw. Snaith struck Cullen's gun wrist before the troubleshooter could clear leather. Cullen cursed as he lost his hold on the weapon. He reached out, grasped a man standing at his side, and thrust him bodily into Snaith. Moran jabbed the muzzle of his pistol against Cullen's short ribs as the man turned to flee.

'Hold it right there,' snapped Moran.

Cullen froze and looked around. He glanced down at Moran's pistol and heaved a long sigh. His resistance faded and he shrugged as he raised his hands.

'What is this all about?' he demanded. 'Are you sure you've got the right man?'

'Let's go along to my office and we'll talk about it,' Snaith replied, wiping beer from his face. He searched

Cullen and found a .41 derringer in an inside pocket of the man's jacket. 'OK. Get moving. You know where the jail is, and don't try any more tricks.'

They took Cullen to the jail and seated him on a chair facing the desk. Snaith stood beside the desk while Moran positioned himself behind Cullen. Davis was seated behind the desk; Moran kept his pistol in his hand. Cullen reached into a pocket, produced a small sack of Bull Durham tobacco and proceeded to roll himself a cigarette. Snaith struck a match, lit the cigarette, and watched Cullen puff contentedly.

'So what is this about?' Cullen demanded at length.

Snaith looked at Moran.

'Explain why you took Trooper Davis to that house up the hill behind the main street,' said Moran.

Cullen half-twisted in his seat and looked up at Moran. 'Who the hell are you?' he demanded.

'Provost Captain Slade Moran. I am handling the investigation into the recent disappearance of the army payroll and escort that left Fort Benson four days ago.'

'So why pick me up? Am I supposed to know something about that?'

'You do, obviously, because you told Trooper Davis you knew where Trooper Ward Price was staying in town, and Price was one of the soldiers guarding the payroll coach when it left Fort Benson. You disarmed Davis, forced him to accompany you and two others to the house where Price was staying and you gave instructions for Davis to be held until Floyd Price could be informed of the situation. You left the house to go to the hotel to check on the mining salesman that Davis said he had ridden into town with – namely me.'

'Who ever told you that story was lying through his teeth, mister,' Cullen responded.

'I was on the porch in front of the hotel when you and two other men passed with Davis,' continued Moran. 'You had hold of Davis by an arm and Kenton was holding a lev-elled gun. I followed you to the house in question and saw and heard everything that took place on the doorstep. When you left to go to the hotel I entered the house and arrested Trooper Price. A man named Sarn was killed when I freed Trooper Davis. I arrested Kenton, and he and Price are in the cells here. So cut out the lying and let us get down to business. I've got you dead to rights, Cullen, and you have no option but to come clean.'

Cullen's expression had slowly taken on a tinge of dis-belief as he listened to Moran's account, and horror showed on his face by the time Moran fell silent.

'So what have you got to say for yourself,' Snaith prompted when Cullen remained silent. 'What have you been up to, Cullen?'

'You tell me,' Cullen replied. 'You seem to know more than I do.'

'Lock him up,' said Moran. 'We'll have Price out here and hear what he has to say.'

Snaith nodded and picked up the cell keys. Moran escorted Cullen to the cells. Snaith locked Cullen in and Price was released from his cell and taken into the office. Price sat down before the desk and folded his arms. His face showed an expression of sullen defiance. He gazed down at the floor and did not look up when Moran spoke to him.

'I want you to give me an account of your movements from the time you left Fort Benson with the payroll escort until I arrested you,' said Moran.

Price heaved a sigh. 'I guess you caught me flat-footed,' he said. 'I'd been planning to desert the army at the first opportunity, and when I was put on the payroll escort unexpectedly I took the chance to get away. When we were clear of the fort I told Sergeant Tully my horse had gone lame and he told me to return for a fresh mount and then catch them up. When they were out of sight I headed here to Moundville, where I've been hiding ever since.'

Moran frowned as he regarded Price, who sat back in his seat and compressed his lips.

'So you know nothing about the coach and payroll going missing,' said Moran.

'As far as I know the escort detail took the coach on to Colorado Springs.' Price grimaced. 'Are you saying they didn't get there?'

'I was with the patrol that found the coach and escort dumped in a derelict mine between here and the trail to Colorado Springs,' said Moran. 'Every man in the escort had been shot in cold blood, the coach had been taken apart and hidden and even the horses had been killed and concealed. The only thing we did not find was the payroll. I don't accept your story that you deserted as soon as you cleared the fort, Price. I think you took part in the slaughter of eight soldiers and that you know what happened to the payroll, and it will be in your best interests to tell the truth and help me with my investigation.'

'Not me!' Price spoke stolidly. 'What do you take me

91

for? The men in the escort were all comrades of mine. I deserted because I couldn't stand any more of army life, and I wouldn't have done what you are suggesting, not in a million years. I swear to God I'm telling the truth.'

'How did you come to be staying in the house where I arrested you?' asked Moran.

'My brother lives there. He is the manager of the Bonanza mine.'

'And you are sure there is nothing you want to tell me before I continue with my investigation?' persisted Moran.

'I've told you all I know.' Price shook his head. 'It was sheer coincidence that someone stole the payroll after I deserted. I'm sorry I can't help you.'

'Was your brother aware that you had deserted?' Moran persisted.

'No.' Price shook his head emphatically. 'I told him I had a week's leave from the fort. He doesn't know the truth. I was going to leave when the week was up and head for Denver instead of returning to the fort.'

Moran glanced at Snaith. The deputy's face was showing tension.

'Is it true that you found those soldiers dead and the payroll missing?' Snaith asked.

Moran nodded. 'I'm afraid so. Put Price back in his cell. I'll talk to him again later, when he's had time to consider his position. We'd better go and talk to Price's brother. If he does know Price is a deserter then he could face a charge of aiding and abetting.'

'I told you he doesn't know a thing about it,' said Price sullenly.

'We shall see.' Moran motioned with his gun. 'Let's get

moving. I have much to do before morning.'

'I'll back you all the way,' said Snaith. . . .

SEVEN

Floyd returned to his house following his appointment with Royston Talmadge, filled with determination to put Kerry Talmadge in his place. He would wait until morning for a confrontation, in case Frint had been telling the truth and Kerry was sick, but in the meantime he intended giving his brother Ward instructions on what to do about Kerry if that son of a bitch was playing a crooked game. He entered his house by the front door, and paused in mid-stride when he caught the unmistakable stink of gunsmoke. He sniffed tentatively, frowned and wondered what was going on.

'Hey, Ward, where are you?' he called.

Silence followed the echo of his voice and he walked to the open door of the back room. His teeth clicked together in shock when he saw Joe Sarn stretched out dead with a pistol by his side and a large stain of blood on his shirt front.

'Jeez!' he gasped, freezing in horror. He did not need to examine Sarn to see if he was dead. The little troubleshooter had been shot through the heart and must

94

have died instantly.

Floyd stirred himself, wondering what had taken place. He called for Ward again, and when there was no response he went through the house making a rapid search half-expecting to find Ward dead. He ascended the stairs to look in the bedrooms, and relief filled him when he failed to find his brother. But where was Ward? Why had he left the house? He descended the stairs, and was startled to see Deputy Sheriff Snaith and a big stranger standing just inside the front door. The stranger was holding a drawn gun.

'What are you doing in here, Snaith?' Floyd demanded. 'I was about to call on you. I came in from the mine a couple of minutes ago, smelled gunsmoke and found Sarn lying shot dead in a back room. Is that why you are here? But how in hell did you know Sarn was dead?'

'We've got your brother in the jail,' said Snaith.

Moran put out his left hand and silenced Snaith. 'I'm Captain Moran, a military investigator,' he said. 'I'll tell you what's going on.'

Floyd gave no outward sign of his feelings. His face remained impassive although panic surged through him like a flash flood. His eyes narrowed and he breathed shallowly through his mouth. Moran, watching him intently, spotted the telltale signs of mental agitation.

'What is your name?' Moran asked quietly.

'Snaith knows my name as well as he knows his own,' Floyd said tensely.

'But I don't know you from Abraham Lincoln so tell me who you are.'

'Floyd Price. I'm the manager of the Bonanza mine.'

'And you have a brother named Ward Price.'

'That's right.' Floyd nodded. 'He's on seven days' leave from Fort Benson.'

'He deserted from Fort Benson five days ago,' Moran corrected, watching Floyd for any change of expression. He saw Floyd's eyes narrow, and noted that the pupils contracted.

'He deserted?' Floyd shook his head emphatically. 'He told me he had leave of absence. I don't believe he deserted. He loves the army.'

'What did he tell you about the missing payroll?' asked Moran.

'He never mentioned a payroll, missing or otherwise. Is that what you're trying to pin on him?'

'I'm not attempting to pin anything on him,' said Moran. 'I'm trying to find out what has been happening around here during the last few days. If your brother has lied to you about his position and intentions then you will have no idea what the situation is. I'll come back to that shortly. But there is another matter you might be able to help me with. You employ a man named Hank Kenton as a troubleshooter for the mine, I believe.'

'That's right. He's not in trouble as well, is he?' Floyd began to breathe a little easier.

Moran noted Floyd's relief. 'What work has Kenton done for the mine during the past five days?' he asked.

'I don't keep a check on the troubleshooters.' Floyd shrugged. 'We employ a man named Rafe Cullen as chief troubleshooter, who has two men working with him. They guard the mine and handle general security to ensure that nothing is stolen by the miners and workers. This week, I

96

believe, they were out tracking down a gang that was trying to get the miners to filch gold nuggets to sell on.'

'Do you have a report of the activities of the troubleshooters?' Moran queried.

'Cullen reports verbally. There was a shoot-out with the gang, and a quantity of gold was recovered. You'd learn a lot more if you spoke to Cullen himself.'

'Rafe Cullen and Hank Kenton are under arrest at the moment, and neither man is prepared to answer questions, apparently fearing that they might incriminate themselves.' Moran glanced at Snaith. 'Is there anything you would like to ask Mr Price?'

'There is.' Snaith straightened his shoulders. 'On whose orders did Cullen, Kenton and Sarn grab a trooper by the name of Davis and bring him to this house as a prisoner?'

'Are you joking?' Floyd was genuinely shocked.

'I overheard Cullen telling your brother Ward to hold Davis here until you could be informed of his presence in town,' added Moran. 'I entered this house to discover Kenton binding Trooper Davis with rope. Sarn drew a gun the instant he saw me and I was forced to shoot him. Can you tell me what orders your troubleshooters had been given? I am assuming they would not act on their own initiative.'

Floyd shook his head. 'I've already told you that I don't control the troubleshooters,' he said impatiently.

'We'll go back to the law office and take statements from the men involved,' Moran said to Snaith. 'Once I get a statement from your brother I shall come and talk to you again, Mr Price. If you do know anything at all about the missing payroll then it will be to your advantage if you speak up voluntarily and not leave it to me to extract an admission from you.'

'Don't leave town, Floyd,' said Snaith harshly.

Floyd heaved a silent sigh of relief when Moran and Snaith had departed. He closed the front door behind them, slid home the bolts and then walked aimlessly through the lower rooms while he tried to get his mind to function normally. But shock was clogging his nerve ends and he did not seem able to think clearly. The knowledge that Sarn was dead and Ward, Cullen and Kenton were in jail lay like a leaden weight in his thoughts. He had believed they were in the clear about the payroll robbery, although he had known the army would come to Moundville, searching and asking questions. So how much did that sharp-eyed Captain Moran know? Or was he merely surmising?

He went into his study and sat down at the desk. His hands were shaking and there was a cold sensation in the pit of his stomach. He reached for a whiskey bottle and swigged from it. When his mind began working smoothly again he considered the situation. It looked as if Ward was in bad trouble. Evidently he had denied any knowledge of the payroll robbery, but was being held as a deserter. Suddenly he felt that the whole business had blown up in his face. What if Ward broke down and admitted organizing the payroll robbery? Would he implicate everyone who had taken part?

A cold sweat broke out on Floyd's forehead and he cuffed it away. Panic assailed him: they would come for him next! He got to his feet, his eyes widening in fear. He had to get away from Moundville. He could cut his losses and run! He sensed that his carefully laid plans had collapsed like a roof fall in an unstable mine shaft, and if he delayed too long he would be caught in the net, which could mean a rope around his neck. He gulped, and fought to override the fear that threatened to swamp him. They wouldn't get him! He could take the payroll from the bank and lose himself somewhere back east. Thirty-eight thousand dollars was not the great wealth he had planned to steal, but it would keep him going until he could work out another plan to get rich.

He made an effort to control his panic. He picked up the whiskey bottle but put it down again without drinking. He needed a clear head now, he had to analyze the situation. As far as he knew there were just three men with some knowledge of what had happened: Snaith, Captain Moran and the trooper, Davis. Floyd began to breathe easier. If they were silenced then the crisis would be over. Excitement filtered through him. If he killed them and released Ward, Cullen and Kenton from the jail they would be back on track, and if Kerry Talmadge toed the line then the big steal would still be on.

Floyd opened a drawer of his desk, took out a pistol and checked it carefully. His fingers trembled with suppressed excitement. This was the only way out. If he acted swiftly then the situation could be retrieved. He filled the pockets of his jacket with .45 shells from a box. Time was fleeting. He had to act decisively and immediately.

He left the house and walked down the hill to the main street. His mind had settled back in its usual cunning groove and his eyes glinted as he considered what he must do. He walked through the shadows to the law office. There was a light in the big front window. The street door was closed. He suppressed a shiver as he imagined what was going on inside the building. He peered through the window and saw Snaith seated behind his desk. Ward was sitting on a chair in front of the desk, and the military investigator was interrogating him and writing down his replies. Ward was shaking his head determinedly, as if denying all accusations. A trooper in uniform was standing in a corner of the office, listening intently to what was being said.

Floyd lifted his pistol. All he had to do was smash the window and start shooting. He had no option but to go ahead with the desperate action because if he did not then he was finished and all his dreams would be down in the dust. He swung the pistol, but paused before crashing the muzzle against the window. Shooting would bring towns-men running, which was the last thing he wanted. He had to break the prisoners out of jail without raising an alarm.

He stood in the shadows and reconsidered. He could not take on three men and kill them silently. If they separated then he had a chance, but it looked as if they were set for the night, trying to get statements from the prisoners. He put his pistol into a pocket, entered the alley beside the jail and felt his way through dense shadows to the rear of the building. A back window glimmered with faint yellow light and he peered through it into the cell block.

A lamp was alight in the cell block, standing on a small shelf just inside the door leading into the law office. The door was closed. Floyd found himself looking directly into a cell, and could see the legs and feet of a man lying on a bunk. The window was too small to permit a man to escape by way of it, and was fixed open a few inches to permit air to circulate. Floyd pressed closer to the glass, craned his neck and called in a hoarse whisper.

'Cullen, can you hear me? It's Floyd.'

There was no reply and he called louder. He saw the feet move on the bunk, and then Hank Kenton stood up and came to the window.

'Who's out there?' demanded Kenton.

'Floyd. What the hell is going on, Kenton? How come you and Cullen got yourselves into this fix?'

'Can you get us out of here?' asked Kenton. 'Snaith is helping a military investigator to get statements from us. They seem to know all about the payroll; they are questioning your brother now. They're holding him for desertion, but they're harping on about the stolen payroll.'

'Has anyone admitted anything?' Floyd demanded.

'Hell, no! What do you take us for? Can you get us out of here? Hold your horses a minute while I tell Cullen you're here.'

Floyd waited in a foment of impatience. He saw Kenton move to the bars separating him from the next cell, and a moment later Rafe Cullen stepped into view. Kenton came back to the window.

'Rafe says if you can slip us a couple of guns we can bust out of here with no trouble,' hissed Kenton.

Floyd produced his pistol and pushed it through the opening until the cylinder jammed between two slats. Kenton grabbed the weapon and jerked it violently until it slipped through the gap.

'Here are some extra slugs.' Floyd passed a handful of cartridges into Kenton's ready hand. 'If you can bust out you'll have to kill Snaith and the two soldiers, and then head up to the mine and hide in my office. I've got a few things to sort out in town but I'll get to you as soon as I can. Stay out of sight and don't attract any attention to yourselves. Tell Cullen we'll be in the clear if Snaith and the two soldiers are killed.'

'See you on the outside,' replied Kenton, and went back to Cullen, who took the pistol and concealed it under the blanket on his bunk.

Floyd moved away. He returned to the street and went on to the hotel. He needed to talk to Kerry Talmadge. At the hotel he peered into the bar and saw Kerry and Cass Frint propping up the bar. Floyd's eyes glinted. Kerry didn't look sick; he was drinking steadily. Frint had a glass of beer before him but was not imbibing. The gunman's gaze was roving as usual, watching his surroundings incessantly, and when he spotted Floyd in the doorway he leaned toward Kerry and whispered. Kerry looked around, saw Floyd and grinned, then turned away. Floyd set his teeth and entered the bar, not liking Kerry's attitude.

'Have you seen Royston, Floyd?' Kerry demanded.

'Frint told me earlier that you were sick,' Floyd said tensely. 'I wish I had your powers of recuperation. What's going on, Kerry? Royston told me he went for your story and signed over the mine to you. He wants me to back you and hopes you'll make a success of the venture. So why didn't you wait to see your father when I could be present? That is what we arranged. Are you trying to work a fast one? You'll be almighty sorry if you are.'

'So you don't trust me!' Kerry laughed. 'Use your sense, Floyd. Why should I want to double-cross you? I don't know where the new vein is, and I need your expertise and money to get at it. I saw Royston alone because I knew I could swing the deal without your help, and I wanted to keep everything simple and natural. It worked like a treat, and tomorrow we can get to work lining our own pockets with gold.'

'It is not going to be that straightforward,' Floyd said. 'We've got trouble.' He explained the situation and saw Kerry's face pale.

'Well what are you doing about it?' Kerry demanded. 'You've got to hit the jail and kill those men before word gets out about the payroll robbery. I thought you said there was no chance of anyone discovering where you had hidden the coach and the dead soldiers. Should I send Frint along to the law office to take care of the lawmen? He won't make any mistakes. He'll take out the law with no trouble.'

'Cullen can handle it. I've passed a gun to him. He'll wait until they let him out of his cell, and when he and the others get clear they'll go up to the mine and hide in my office. By morning the crisis will have passed. I have every faith in Cullen.'

Frint was watching Floyd like a hungry wolf. Eagerness was showing in his eyes.

'We've got a goldmine to run now.' Kerry sounded worried. 'We want everything to be straightforward. Sort out this trouble before morning, Floyd. Kill your own men, if you have to, to shut their mouths. Have you thought of that?'

'One of them is my brother, and there's no way I'll kill him,' Floyd retorted.

Kerry shrugged. 'Just remember that I'm in the clear,' he said. 'I had no part in stealing the payroll or killing the soldiers. So you'd better act quickly and stop the rot before word gets out. Where is the payroll? We'll need some of that dough quickly to open up the new vein. You'd better give me the location of the vein in case anything happens to you. And who are the miners you can trust to keep their mouths shut? There's a lot to be worked out, Floyd, and we need to get started at once.'

'The crisis will be over before morning.' Floyd spoke through clenched teeth. He didn't like how Kerry was whitewashing himself. If they went down then they would all drop together. Floyd opened his mouth to say so, but saw that Frint was watching him closely and changed his mind. He could always get at Kerry if he needed to. Right now he had to concentrate on the law office and what was going on inside it.

'Have you got a spare gun?' he asked. 'I passed mine into the jail. I'm gonna have to stand by there and help out when my men make their bid to escape. If I can catch any of the lawmen alone I'll kill them.'

'Well that's your problem.' Kerry glanced at the watchful Frint. 'Have you got a spare gun you can give Floyd?'

Frint reached into his left armpit, produced a short-barrelled .44 Remington, and passed it over to Floyd, who dropped it into a pocket of his coat.

'It's hair-triggered,' Frint advised. 'Mind you don't shoot yourself with it.'

'Be at the mine office early tomorrow morning,' said Floyd. 'We've got some details of partnership to sort out before we set to work, so don't drink too much tonight.'

He turned and departed, his mind filled with what he had to do. He walked back to the law office and stood in the alley beside it, hunched in the shadows, motionless and deadly. He eased forward and peered through the front window of the office, saw that Ward was still being questioned and forced himself to wait patiently for the situation to change in his favour. He could only watch for Cullen to be brought out to be questioned, and be ready to support his chief troubleshooter when that moment arrived.

As time passed, Floyd grew restless. Impatience gnawed at him as he considered how delicately his plans were balanced. A slight movement either way could see him coming out on top or failing. He peered through the front window of the office again, and stiffened when he saw that Snaith had got up from his desk. The deputy picked up his bunch of keys and led the way into the cells, followed by Ward and the trooper, who drew his pistol and covered Ward.

Floyd waited tensely, and a sigh of disappointment escaped him when Snaith and the soldier emerged from the cell block without another of the prisoners. The connecting door was locked. Snaith threw the bunch of keys on the desk and the trooper sat down behind the desk to write a report. Snaith came towards the street door and opened it. He paused in the doorway and half turned to speak.

'I'll make a round of the town and then go for supper,

Captain,' he said. 'I'll be as quick as I can.'

Floyd eased back into deeper shadow. He heard the office door close. When he risked a look along the street he saw Snaith walking away from him and slipped out of his cover to follow. Excitement filled him as he put a hand into his pocket and grasped the gun Frint had given him. He would let Snaith get to the far end of the street and then nail him. With the deputy out of the way it would be much easier to handle the two soldiers back there in the law office.

Snaith progressed along the street, checking doors and trying windows. He did not look left or right as he continued with the boring chore, using only a part of his mind as he followed his habitual route. His thoughts were filled with the investigation going on about the missing payroll, He was certain the prisoners in the jail were guilty, and wondered who else would be pulled in to answer charges. It looked like being a big case, and some of the miners were involved. He moved on faster, eager to get back to the office and watch the investigation unfold. Captain Moran certainly knew his job.

Floyd followed the deputy like a black shadow, and, when Snaith disappeared into the darkness at the end of the street to check out the livery barn, he moved in silently. He heard a door rattle as Snaith shook it and stepped in behind a front corner of the building. Snaith was retracing his steps. He stopped a couple of feet from the corner to try a small window. Floyd took the pistol from his pocket and cocked it. Snaith evidently heard the sound for he swung round and dropped his right hand to the butt of his holstered gun.

'Who's there?' Snaith demanded. He stepped away from the window and looked around as if trying to decide on the direction from which the sound had come.

Floyd kept close to the corner and eased forward, his gun hand ready. He saw Snaith's outline, took aim and squeezed the trigger of the small gun. The crack of the shot hammered and the weapon recoiled in Floyd's hand. Snaith uttered a cry and pitched over backwards. He hit the ground heavily and did not move again. Floyd looked around, wondering if the shot had been heard. He smothered a wild impulse to flee the scene and forced himself to approach Snaith. He bent over the deputy and pressed a hand against Snaith's chest. There was no heartbeat. Floyd grinned and straightened. He slid back around the corner and faded into the shadows. One down and two to go, he told himself as he made his way back to the law office. . . .

EIGHT

Moran leaned back in his seat and looked up at Trooper Davis. He shook his head as Davis opened his mouth to ask a question.

'We'll call it a day now,' said Moran. 'The prisoners need time to think about their situation so we'll come back to them in the morning. You get away now, Davis. Report back here tomorrow at eight o'clock. You'll try to get a bed at the general store tonight, won't you?'

'I could, Captain. They'll sure put me up. But I don't think I could face Dora knowing Biddle is dead. I couldn't look her in the eyes. I'll bed down in the stable. I've done it before. I can sneak up to the hayloft.'

'Off you go, then.' Moran glanced at the clock on the wall. 'I'll wait for the deputy to get back before I go to the hotel.'

'Goodnight, sir.' Davis departed and closed the door. He paused on the sidewalk to look around the street. Moundville seemed to have gone to sleep. There were lights in most of the houses but the main street was deserted. He decided to get a meal and walked along to the diner, unaware that Floyd Price stepped out of the alley beside the law office and followed him.

The restaurant was busy. Davis sat down at a table opposite the door. Two waitresses were serving and were being run off their feet. Davis knew them both by sight from his previous visits to the town. One of them, Rose Dugdale, finally stopped by his table.

'Hello, soldier,' she greeted. 'How long have you been in town?'

'Hi, Rose. I got in today.'

'Did Ray Biddle come with you? Dora is getting mighty excited about the wedding.'

'Ray couldn't get away this time.' Davis frowned as he pictured Biddle dead in the derelict mine. 'But he'll be here in time for the wedding, you can bet.'

Floyd entered the diner and came to Davis's table.

'Mind if I sit here?' he asked.

'I don't mind,' Davis replied. He gave Rose an order and relaxed.

'It is mighty busy in here this evening,' observed Floyd.

'We don't often see you in here, Mr Price,' Rose countered.

Davis glanced at Floyd, noted the town suit and guessed he was not an ordinary miner. The name Price struck him forcibly. Was this the brother of Ward Price?

'You're right,' Floyd replied, smiling at Rose 'I didn't get finished at the mine until late, and it was too much trouble to cook a meal at home.'

'Is there any truth in the rumour that the mine is petering out?' asked Rose.

Floyd smiled and shook his head. 'I don't know how

109

rumours start, but there is no truth in that one. Bring me a steak with all the trimmings, Rose.'

Rose departed. Floyd glanced at Davis.

'You're a long way from the fort, soldier,' he commented.

'I've got a pass.' Davis shrugged. 'Moundville isn't much but it is better than Fort Benson. So you work up at the mine.'

'I'm the general manager,' replied Floyd.

Davis did not bat an eyelid at the information. This was the brother of Ward Price – the man Cullen had mentioned about seeing before ordering Davis to be killed. Davis wondered if Floyd's presence in the diner was a coincidence or premeditated. He gave no outward sign of his thoughts but alerted himself to possible danger.

'I've never seen a goldmine,' Davis said. 'What is it like working in one?'

Floyd grimaced and then smiled. His eyes glinted. 'You'd be well advised to stick to soldiering. But if you'd like to look around the workings I'll take you up there and show you how it all works.'

'Thanks, but no thanks. I have to be back at the fort in a couple of days and I don't want to waste a moment of my time.'

'You're a wise man.' Floyd studied Davis's face while the soldier was looking around the diner, and came to the conclusion that luck was giving him a break. Snaith was dead and now one of the two soldiers was out of the jail and just asking to be picked off. 'Where are you staying in town?' he asked. 'Do you have friends around?'

'I'll hit the sack in the livery barn after I've eaten,' said

Davis. 'I do have friends in town, but I'd rather not stay with them.'

'A hayloft is no place for a soldier on leave.' Floyd shook his head. 'I've got plenty of room at my house. You're welcome to spend the night there.'

'That's kind of you, but no thanks. I guess I'm in a rut when it comes to living rough.'

Floyd nodded. He looked around the diner and their conversation petered out. When their meals arrived they ate silently, and when Floyd had finished eating he arose from the table.

'See you around, soldier,' he said. 'Enjoy your leave.'

'Thanks, I will,' Davis responded, and watched Floyd's departure with a narrowed gaze.

Davis left the diner minutes later and went to a saloon for a drink. He did not stay long and departed to head for the livery barn. He paused in the dense shadows by the big front door to glance around, and then sneaked into the building. He waited until his eyes became accustomed to the gloom before moving to the ladder giving access to the hayloft. He began to ascend, and was startled by a black shadow which lunged at him from his right. He lifted his right arm to fend off an attack but the butt of a pistol slammed against his forehead with stunning force. He fell backward off the bottom rung of the ladder, and lost consciousness when the pistol struck him again.

Floyd paused with his pistol raised for a third blow, but realized that it was not needed; Davis lay crumpled at his feet. A sense of exultation gripped Floyd; this was working out better than he had hoped. He dragged Davis into an empty stall, searched around for a lariat and then bound the unconscious soldier and gagged him with his own neckerchief. He left the stable quickly and hurried back along the street to the law office. Now there was only one man guarding the prisoners, and Floyd was certain his way was clear at last.

The light shining in the law office window drew Floyd like a moth to a flame. He sneaked in close and peered through the dusty glass. Captain Moran was pacing the office. Floyd grinned, his brain working fast. He reached out a hand, tried the door of the office, and it opened to his touch. He entered. Moran swung around, his hand making an instinctive movement towards the butt of the pistol in the cutaway holster on his cartridge belt, and he half-drew the weapon before changing his mind and thrusting it back into leather.

'Excuse me butting in, Captain,' said Floyd. 'I'm worried about my brother Ward. May I see him for a couple of minutes?'

Moran gazed at Floyd to gauge his attitude, and decided that he presented no danger. Floyd did not seem to be armed, and had both hands in plain view.

'I'm sorry, but you can't see him,' Moran replied. 'He's under interrogation.'

'You're holding him as a deserter, huh?' Floyd shrugged. 'I don't see why that should prevent me seeing him. I need to know if there is anything he wants.'

Floyd looked toward the desk, and his eyes glinted when he saw a bunch of keys lying there. He returned his gaze to Moran's face, his expression bland, and a pleading note crept into his voice as he repeated his request to see his brother. He saw Moran shake his head, and put his right hand into his coat pocket. His fingers closed around the butt of the pistol nestling there, and he steeled himself for action.

'I work to a set of rules,' said Moran, 'and I cannot break them. The book says to keep all suspects incommunicado until an investigation ends, and you won't be permitted to see your brother until I have obtained a confession from him, for I have reason to believe he is involved in a crime.'

'What is there to confess about desertion? He is absent without leave or he isn't.'

'There's no doubt about his desertion.' Moran kept his hand close to the butt of his holstered pistol. 'He admitted that much too easily for my liking. I am of the opinion that he pleaded guilty to the lesser crime of desertion in order to escape suspicion of being involved in much more serious charges.'

'What other charges?' Floyd could feel sweat breaking out on his forehead as he began to lift the pistol from his pocket.

'I'm afraid I cannot discuss the case with you.' Moran shook his head firmly. 'Now I must ask you to leave. If you come back some time tomorrow you may be permitted to see your brother then.'

Floyd shrugged and half-turned toward the street door. His eyes did not leave Moran and, when Moran switched his attention to the desk, Floyd took the pistol from his pocket and levelled it. The clicks of the weapon being cocked attracted Moran's gaze. He reached instinctively for his holstered gun, but stayed the movement when he saw the black muzzle of Floyd's gun covering him.

'Get your hands up,' snarled Floyd. 'This gun is hair-triggered, so do like you're told.'

Moran lifted his hands. His eyes glinted as he gauged Floyd's attitude, and he realized that he was standing on the threshold of eternity, for Floyd looked deadly serious.

'You're making a big mistake,' said Moran. 'The deputy will be back soon. If you have any sense at all you'll put away your gun and get out of here.'

'Just shut your mouth. Turn around so I can disarm you. Don't think I won't shoot you. I killed that deputy when he left here to do his evening round, so you could wait till hell freezes over and wouldn't see him. And you won't get any help from that trooper who was here with you. I've got him hogtied in the livery barn. Now do like I tell you.'

Moran turned his back on Floyd, his muscles tensed in anticipation of a shot. He was shocked by Floyd's admission of killing Snaith. He felt Floyd's fingers grasp the butt of his gun and jerk it from the holster.

'That's better,' said Floyd. 'Now pick up those cell keys and use them. Turn my brother and my two troubleshooters loose.'

Moran moved reluctantly but with a gun covering his back he had no choice but to obey. He picked up the cell keys and led the way into the cell block. Ward Price got up off his bunk and came to the door of his cell when he saw Moran, and let out a whoop of joy when he saw Floyd with two levelled guns.

'What are you waiting for?' Floyd demanded. 'Unlock the cells.'

Moran unlocked the door of Ward's cell. Floyd handed

Moran's pistol to his brother.

'Keep him covered, Ward,' Floyd instructed. He snatched the bunch of keys from Moran's hand and released Cullen and Kenton.

Cullen emerged from his cell with the gun Floyd had passed through the window. He struck Moran with the gun. Moran dropped to his knees. Cullen cocked the pistol.

'No shooting in here,' Floyd rapped. 'Save it for later. Cut along to the livery barn, Kenton, and pick up the trooper I left hogtied there. He's in a stall. Bring him along to my house, and don't let anyone see you. Cullen, you and Ward take Moran to my house. Let's get out of here by the back door, and keep to the shadows.'

Cullen dragged Moran to his feet and pushed him toward the back of the jail. Floyd took the cell keys from Cullen and unlocked the back door. Kenton departed quickly and vanished into the shadows at the rear of the jail. Floyd looked around, grinning. It had been all too easy. He walked through to the law office, locked the street door on the inside, and then returned to the cells. Cullen was waiting at the back doorway. Ward was standing in the background with a big grin on his face. Moran stood with his hands raised, and Cullen nudged him with the muzzle of his pistol.

'OK, Captain,' said Cullen. 'You know the way to Floyd's house so get moving. Try and get the better of me, if you fancy your chances.'

'I told you no shooting,' Floyd warned. 'Take him up to the house and hold him there until I get back. I've got some business to handle but I won't be long. Keep a close eye on things, Ward. When Kenton shows up with that trooper, hogtie both prisoners and keep them quiet. We'll dispose of them in one of the search tunnels in the mine, and no one will ever know they came to Moundville.'

Cullen menaced Moran with his pistol and they faded into the shadows with Ward tagging along behind.

Floyd locked the rear door of the jail and went to the back lots. He tossed the cell keys into the darkness as he made his way to Willard Bodeen's house next to the bank; he needed to collect the stolen payroll from the banker. When he knocked at Bodeen's front door he was surprised when it was opened almost immediately by the banker, who seemed to be in a highly nervous state.

'Floyd, I'm glad it's you,' said Bodeen. 'I was going to send for you. I want that payroll money removed from the bank.'

'I'm here to collect it,' Floyd replied. 'You look all shook up, Will. Have you been worrying about that money?'

'I haven't been able to sleep nights since it came into the bank,' said Bodeen. 'I was a fool to agree going in with you. That money could ruin me if it was found in the bank.'

'It doesn't look any different to any other money.' Floyd laughed. 'I suppose you want me to give you the shortfall caused by that robbery you suffered.'

'That was the deal. Four thousand dollars will cover it.' Bodeen produced a white handkerchief and mopped his brow.

Floyd frowned, not liking Bodeen's manner. 'Come on, let's get the dough out of the bank,' he said. 'Then you can forget all about it and stop worrying.'

'I'll get the keys. We'd better go into the bank by the back door. Come on in.'

Bodeen disappeared into the house and Floyd followed him. They entered a study and Bodeen collected his keys before leading the way to the back door of the house, clutching the bank keys in his hand. Floyd followed him silently, filled with doubt and concerned by Bodeen's attitude. He did not think Bodeen would stand up to any questioning that might come his way when the army arrived in greater numbers. Captain Moran seemed to be one smart investigator, and there would be others to take his place when the captain failed to reappear on the scene.

They entered the bank and Bodeen produced the payroll. Floyd made a great show of counting the money, and Bodeen fussed around him like a wet hen, talking fast in a high-pitched tone, his hands fluttering and waving impatiently.

'You don't need to count it, Floyd,' Bodeen protested. 'Just give me four thousand dollars and take the rest out of my sight.'

Floyd counted the money out of one of the bulging sacks and handed it over. Bodeen locked it in the safe.

'Don't come to me with any more of your schemes,' said Bodeen. 'I want no more of your business. I'll still handle Bonanza business, but I want nothing further to do with you.'

'OK, if that's how you feel about it.' Floyd hefted the sacks across his shoulder. 'We'll both forget about this, so no talking about it, Will.'

Bodeen heaved a sigh and opened the back door a fraction to peer out into the shadows. He stepped aside and motioned for Floyd to depart. Floyd went off without a backward glance, and heard Bodeen locking the back door of the bank as he strode up the hill toward his house. He felt highly satisfied with the way his problems had worked themselves out, and if he could get a good response from Kerry Talmadge in the morning then the next part of his scheme should unfold relatively smoothly. . . .

In the hotel bar, Kerry Talmadge was drinking more than was good for him, and Cass Frint was doing his utmost to prevent his young boss from drinking himself under the table. He had tried hinting without success, and when he spoke outright about the amount Kerry was putting away, Kerry blew his top, as he always did.

'Why don't you shut up and find another place to drink in?' demanded Kerry. 'Who appointed you nursemaid to me? You're only a bodyguard, so don't try to overstep the mark or you'll be out of a job. I'm old enough to make my own decisions, thank you, so butt out.'

'You've got to go up to the mine in the morning and you'll need to have all your wits about you,' Frint replied, getting to his feet. 'If you drink too much tonight Floyd will run rings around you tomorrow, and no way will you be able to better him. He plays a mean game. But if you don't mind losing your shirt to him then go right ahead. I'm through talking. I'll butt out all right, and see how you make out on your own.'

'Shut up and stay where you are. What do you think I pay you for?'

'You're beginning to sound more and more like your old man,' scoffed Frint. 'It's about time you learned to stand on your own feet. You're not going to play square with Floyd, are you?'

'I can't do anything but mind my manners until I learn where he's keeping that payroll,' replied Kerry. 'It'll be a different story once I get my hands on that. However tomorrow is another day, and I'll put one over on mighty clever Floyd Price before this is over.'

Frint shrugged. He couldn't care less what happened to this latest scheme that Kerry was involved in. All he knew was that it was crooked, and his interest extended only as far as the size of the bonus he would collect. He sat down and watched Kerry drinking steadily. This way of life was becoming monotonous, he realized. Perhaps it was time to consider changing his job; the payroll Floyd was holding would make a suitable severance bonus. . . .

Floyd returned to his house and Ward opened the front door to him. They went into the study. Floyd dumped the sacks containing the payroll on the desk.

'Is that the payroll?' asked Ward.

'It is, and it will get us started in our new business.' Floyd glanced around the study. 'I need somewhere safe to leave this while we get rid of the two prisoners. Don't let Cullen and Kenton know the money is here. It could be too much of a temptation for them.'

'They've got Moran and Davis hogtied,' said Ward. 'What are we gonna do with them? I won't feel safe until they are dead. I stand to get my neck stretched if either of them passes on the word that I'm alive.'

'We'll take them up to the mine in about an hour's

time,' Floyd replied. 'They'll be safe enough in a branch tunnel until tomorrow, and then we'll blast the roof down on them when the morning shift is working. Let's have a drink. No word of your arrest has gotten out from the law office so we are in the clear. I killed the deputy earlier, and there are no witnesses left. You'd better stick close to me from now on, Ward. I may need your help with Kerry Talmadge. I have a sneaking feeling he's planning to double-cross me. Have your gun ready at all times.'

Ward nodded. 'I'll be right behind you.'

Royston Talmadge sat in his study in the big house and drank whiskey intermittently. He wrestled with a doubt that had evolved in his mind since his meeting with Kerry that afternoon and had continued to grow the more he thought about it. A big cigar was clamped between his fleshy lips, and he puffed furiously, his face twisted into an expression of intense concentration. His coach driver and constant companion, Matt Gedge, was seated opposite, holding a glass of whiskey which he hardly touched. Gedge was a powerful man, stocky, bullet-headed, with a square chin and a sharply pointed nose. His pale eyes glimmered as he watched Royston struggling with some deep-rooted problem.

'What's biting you, Boss?' Gedge demanded at length. 'I've never seen you like this before. If a problem comes up you usually know what to do without puzzling over it.'

Royston broke off his train of thought and looked up. His lips twisted as if he had a bad taste in his mouth which he couldn't swallow. 'Did I ask you for your opinion?' he asked. 'Where do you get off, sticking your nose into my private thoughts? Is that what I pay you for? You keep your mind on your duties. Is the coach ready to roll tomorrow?'

'You know it is or you wouldn't ask,' Gedge countered. He got up and poured more whiskey into Royston's glass. 'So what's on your mind? You might as well spill it now. I've never known you keep anything to yourself when the chips are down. You don't have to tell me that it has to do with Kerry. That's a certainty. He's always been a trial to you. I've never known him to do anything right.'

'I've got a smell of trouble in my nostrils.' Royston gulped whiskey and banged the glass on the desk. 'It's a gut feeling, and you know my hunches never fool me. Something is going on right under my nose. I'm being played for a sucker, and I can feel it sure as hens lay eggs.'

Gedge grimaced. 'You never go off half-cocked, so something must have triggered you.'

'That's what's bothering me.' Royston puffed savagely on his cigar. 'The feeling sneaked into my mind while Kerry was talking to me this afternoon. It wasn't what he said that caught me, or his manner. But something didn't ring true. I went along with his proposal because he is my flesh and blood. If a man can't trust his own son then who in hell can he rely on? Then Floyd Price showed up this evening, and there was something in his manner which screamed deceit at me. Floyd plays his cards close to his vest, so he must be planning something big – like stealing off me. Kerry and Floyd were always like cat and dog; they couldn't stand the sight of each other, but these past months they've become thicker than molasses. Something bad is going on right under my nose, Matt, and I can't put my finger on it.'

'You signed over Bonanza to Kerry, didn't you?' Gedge grimaced. 'Your son ain't the kind to get his hands dirty, not even for a fortune, so he's probably got Floyd to do his dirty work for him. Floyd is an ambitious man. When he overheats he sweats ambition. I'd say he is behind anything your son is trying to pull.'

'And it is too damn easy to work out what they are after,' said Royston. 'For weeks Floyd has been sending me negative reports on the mine. The rich vein is petering out; a mountain stream above the mine cut into a rift and went underground; the stream was diverted, but the rift cut right through the gold vein, which began to peter out on the other side of it; the mine is played out because Floyd has dug nine experimental tunnels and come up with nothing new. So I'm cutting my losses and getting out, but I have a nasty suspicion that a new vein has been found and Floyd is keeping it secret.'

'How can you find out?' asked Gedge.

'There is one man who might know – Pete Milligan. He's the top miner on the payroll. You know where he lives, Matt, so go and fetch him. We'll see what we can learn from him. Get moving. You're wasting time. If Milligan can tell me anything then we shall be busy for most of tonight, searching Bonanza for that new vein. The afternoon shift will finish at eight and there will be only a night watchman up at the mine until four in the morning.'

Gedge departed instantly. Royston remained hunched at the desk, drinking copiously, his face screwed up in concentration and his brow furrowed. He remained motionless until he heard a door bang, and straightened in his seat as Gedge ushered Pete Milligan into the study.

'Sit down, Pete,' said Royston. 'Help yourself to a drink.'

'Thank you, Mr Talmadge.' Milligan poured himself a liberal tot of whiskey and sat down. He smiled at Royston, but his eyes showed a certain wariness that registered with the mine owner.

'It isn't good news about Bonanza, Pete,' said Royston. 'The rich vein is about played out and I expect the mine will close down in a few weeks. What do you plan to do when you're paid off?'

Milligan almost choked on his drink as Royston's words sank into his brain.

'Bonanza finished?' he spluttered. 'That ain't what I've been told, Mr Talmadge.'

'So what have you been told, and by whom?' demanded Royston.

'I heard that Kerry plans to take over the mine, with your permission, and carry on searching for a new vein. I think there is still a lot of gold in Bonanza. In fact, I'd stake my life on it.'

'No.' Royston shook his head emphatically. 'Floyd has pretty well exhausted all the possibilities. You know it costs a lot of money to seek gold, and I'm not prepared to waste dough on an outside chance of hitting a new vein. Kerry is taking over here, but he won't get any money from me for development, and he knows that. So it is fairly simple to work out that he must know of the existence of a new vein, and in a couple of weeks, after I have pulled out, it will begin to yield another fortune, but not for me. Is that what is going on, Pete? You wouldn't hold out on me if you knew anything about a scheme like that, would you? We go back a long way, feller, and I like to think that you are one of the very few men around here who would look after my interests.'

'Of course, Mr Talmadge, you can stake your life on me.' Milligan twisted his whiskey glass in suddenly nervous hands. 'I wouldn't go against you for all the gold in the world.'

'That's nice to know, Pete.' Royston nodded. 'Did you oversee the search tunnels that were dug? You are the top miner at Bonanza, so I guess you would have handled that.'

'Yes, sir, I did. And there was one tunnel in particular that I thought looked likely, but we stopped working on it because of a bad fault overhead that made it too dangerous to continue.'

'That sounds interesting,' Royston smiled. 'How about taking Gedge and me up to the mine and showing me that tunnel?'

'You're the boss,' said Milligan. 'When would you like to go?'

'The shift finishes in about an hour.'

'I'd have to get Floyd's permission,' said Milligan. 'He gave strict orders that no one, but no one, should go into that area.'

'I don't think we need bother Floyd with a little matter like that,' observed Royston. 'I'll take full responsibility, seeing that I own Bonanza. Make yourself comfortable for an hour, Pete. I have a feeling it is going to be a long, hard night.'

NINE

The afternoon shift at Bonanza started work at noon and streamed out of the mine at eight in the evening; the stamp mill ceased its monotonous pounding and silence returned to Moundville after sixteen hours of crushing ore. The morning shift would report for work at four in the morning and the whole sequence would recommence. Royston Talmadge stood at the window of his study and watched the fifty or so men passing his house on the way to their homes in the town. Matt Gedge was seated beside the mine owner's big desk, watching a nervous Pete Milligan getting more and more uneasy as the minutes passed.

'What's wrong, Pete?' Gedge asked at length. 'You're beginning to look like a cat up a gum tree with a couple of hounds dogs sleeping underneath. What's biting you, huh?'

'I'm OK,' said Milligan. 'It's just that Floyd made it clear that no one should go into that dangerous tunnel without his say-so. I don't want to get on the wrong side of Floyd – it could cost me my job. So why don't I go down to his

125

house and tell him what we are going to do? Then everyone will be happy.'

Royston turned from the window and slammed a ponderous fist on his desk, making Milligan jump in shock.

'You'll do like I tell you without all the back-biting, Milligan. I've been paying you top wages for years. Didn't I buy your loyalty with your sweat? Here I am trying to save the mine from closing, from throwing a hundred men out of work and turning Moundville into a ghost town, and all you can think of is your own future. So what gives? It looks to me like there is more at stake here than appears on the surface, so you'd better come clean, because if I catch you out it'll be more than your job you'll lose. So what have you got to say?'

'Honest, Boss, I don't know what you're talking about,' Milligan replied uneasily. 'Floyd is my immediate boss and I have to obey his orders. Anything he tells me I believe comes straight from you, so my loyalty doesn't come into it.'

'But I'm telling you here and now that I suspect something bad is going on and I expect you to back me up to the hilt or get the hell out,' grated Royston. 'You can't be on both sides of the fence. Either you are for me or you are against me. So which is it?'

'I'm for you, Boss,' Milligan replied without hesitation.

'Then shut your mouth and look happy about what you are going to do. I can't trust you any longer, Milligan. Matt, you watch him, huh, and if he looks like changing his mind about going along with us then you've got my permission to shoot him.'

'OK,' Gedge grinned as he pulled a short-barrelled

pistol out of a shoulder holster. 'You heard the boss,' he said to Milligan. 'I'll be watching you every minute from here on in.'

'Let's get moving,' said Royston. 'I want to know what's going on in Bonanza, and I need all the answers before morning.'

Gedge waggled his gun in Milligan's face. 'You lead the way,' he suggested, 'and you better pray that I don't trip up behind you because this gun is hair-triggered, and so am I.'

Milligan did not reply. His expression was grim as he left the house and headed up the path to the mine entrance, closely followed by Gedge. Royston proved to be extremely agile for a man of his weight and bulk, and had no problems keeping up with them. When they reached a cluster of wooden shacks built near the mine entrance, Royston called a halt.

'There's a night watchman somewhere around,' he said. 'I know he usually sleeps right through the night so let us make sure he's hit the sack before we continue. I don't want anyone to know what we are doing. Matt, take a peek in that shack on the left. That's where the watchman will be. Milligan, stand where you are, and be warned that I have a gun in my pocket and I'll use it if you give me cause to.'

They stood in the shadows while Gedge went off. After a few moments, he returned.

'The watchman hasn't wasted any time,' Gedge reported. 'He's already snoring.'

'So get on with it, Milligan,' said Royston. 'You lead the way.'

Milligan went forward and passed through the mine entrance, which was illuminated by two kerosene-soaked torches fixed to the walls of the tunnel. Just inside the entrance, the handles of a number of pine torches stuck out of a bucket filled with coal oil, and they each took one, shook off the surplus kerosene, and ignited them. The entrance tunnel was six feet high and four feet wide. Milligan went forward without hesitation, walking quickly, his torch held shoulder-high. The tunnel declined slightly for some sixty yards to a vertical shaft. A wooden ladder had been fixed to the wall of the shaft. Gedge descended first and covered Milligan when the miner descended. Royston found it hard going but moved quickly.

They reached the second level and Milligan again took the lead. There were branch tunnels at intervals along the main tunnel, showing that an intense search had been made to find another vein of gold. Milligan ignored the branch tunnels and went on eagerly, apparently having accepted the situation.

'Now I'm down here I want to take a look at the main vein that is supposed to be petering out,' said Royston. 'Make for it, Milligan.'

The miner continued until he reached a place where the rock floor had been covered over by thick boards. He halted and held his torch high.

'This is where the mountain stream came through,' he said, standing on the boards. 'It flooded right through here until Floyd diverted it. When we dried it out I went down the funnel that the stream had left, maybe a hundred feet, to check for a new vein, but there was nothing doing. I dropped a rock from where I stopped

128

and never heard it hit the bottom.' He pointed upward and Royston saw a circular hole in the roof of the tunnel which had been worn smooth by countless years of tumbling water. 'That's where the stream came in and cut through the main vein. The vein continued on the far side of the rift but is much smaller, as if the water had diverted it over the years. And it is low grade stuff we are getting out now. The end is only fifty yards on from here.'

He went on to the end of the tunnel and stood beside Gedge while Royston inspected the workings. Royston grunted when he saw a stratum of white quartz, merely a foot high and only inches wide. He took up a discarded pick-axe and worked on the stratum, breaking it down before bending closer to examine it for traces of gold.

'It's petered out real bad,' observed Royston. 'Back on the other side of where the stream came through, the stratum was a yard high and three feet wide, with great veins and clusters of gold. OK. So Floyd was telling the truth about the main vein dying on us. So where is the search tunnel where you think he might have struck a new vein, Milligan?'

'We'll have to go back a way. It's off to the right, and heads in a different direction to this tunnel.'

'Show me.' Royston motioned for Gedge to follow Milligan and they retraced their steps to a branch tunnel, their torches creating uncertain light and dense shadows that swirled and danced around them as they progressed.

'In here,' said Milligan at length. He untied a rope that hung across the entrance of a branch tunnel bearing a sign which read, DANGER, FALLING ROOF. KEEP OUT.

The branch tunnel was smaller than the main tunnel,

and Royston cursed when he banged his head. Milligan reached the end of it after some forty yards.

'There is a reason why Floyd said this tunnel is unsafe and banned everyone from coming in here,' said Milligan, 'When Floyd wouldn't let me work in here I came in on the quiet and found what you are looking for.'

Royston held his torch closer to the blank end wall and examined the rock closely.

'There is nothing here to indicate the presence of a vein,' he said. 'So what are you talking about, Milligan?'

Milligan grinned in the faltering light, his teeth gleaming. 'How about this then?' he demanded, pointing to the side wall some six feet back from the end of the tunnel.

Royston leaned forward and thrust his torch close to the wall. He muttered an oath when he saw a stratum of white quartz about three feet wide and roughly two feet in height, which was richly laced with glinting veins and threads of gold.

'Hell, that looks mighty good!' gasped Royston. 'It's one helluva strike.'

'Look in the opposite wall,' said Milligan, holding his torch higher. 'Floyd cut laterally right through the vein. 'See; it goes in two directions, and it sure is high grade.'

'So now we know.' Royston breathed hard. 'There is a double-cross! Floyd made this strike and is keeping quiet about it. And Kerry must be in on the deal. He was telling me only this afternoon that he fancied there was more gold in here, and I believed him when he said he wanted to knuckle down and start working for a living, when all the time he was playing me for a sucker and planning to take Bonanza off me. OK, I've seen enough. Let's get out of here. I want to see Floyd and Kerry in my office at the house as soon as possible. Gedge, it's your job to see that they turn up.'

'Sure, Boss.' Gedge grinned. He half-turned away, his gun momentarily swinging away from Milligan, and he accidentally placed himself between Milligan and Royston.

Milligan had been waiting for just such an opportunity and thrust his burning torch into Gedge's face. Gedge yelped in shock and ducked away. Milligan kept moving, filled with desperation. He kicked Gedge in the stomach and Gedge fell to the ground. Milligan stamped on Gedge's gun arm as he turned to Royston. He thrust the flaming torch against the front of Royston's coat as he kicked Royston in the stomach. The next instant Milligan was running back out of the tunnel, holding his torch high to light his way.

Royston fell to the ground. His coat was alight and he beat at the flames. Gedge rolled over and got to one knee, fingers scrabbling for his dropped gun. He found it, and triggered two shots at the retreating Milligan, who fell instantly and lay still. The shots filled the tunnel with gun thunder and the air seemed to vibrate with shock waves. A piece of rock fell from the roof of the tunnel and struck Royston on the arm. He looked up in alarm as a shower of small rocks fell on him.

'Hey, this place is dangerous!' yelled Royston. 'Don't fire that gun again, Gedge. You'll bring the whole roof down on us.'

Gedge got to his feet. He looked up at the roof of the tunnel. The gun echoes were fading but he heard a more ominous sound in the background, which grew in volume

131

as he listened.

'Come on, Boss,' he yelled, grasping Royston's shoulder and trying to drag him to his feet. 'The roof sounds like it is falling in. Let's get the hell out of here.'

Royston struggled up, filled with panic. He could hear a pit prop groaning as pressure built up on it. More rocks fell from the tunnel roof and the rumbling sound increased.

'Run for your life, Gedge,' Royston yelled. 'The whole place is coming down.'

Gedge needed no second telling. He ran for the main shaft, leaving Royston to follow as best he could. Royston forced his legs into motion and lumbered back the way he had come. A prop suddenly snapped with a noise like a cracking whip, only a yard in front of the mine owner. It splintered under overwhelming pressure and fell in front of Royston, who blundered over it, unable to stop his headlong rush. He could hear rocks falling into the tunnel at his back and forced himself to his feet and lumbered on. His legs seemed to have taken on a will of their own and would not obey his mental command to keep running. Sweat poured down his fleshy face; his heart pounded erratically. Stabbing pains lanced through his chest and he had to fight for breath.

Royston saw Gedge's torch ahead, and tried to increase his speed. A rock struck his left shoulder almost knocking him to his knees. He half-fell, cannoned into the wall of the tunnel and was flung forward on suddenly failing legs. He saw Gedge standing in the main shaft, frantically beckoning him on, and threw his weight forward desperately, trying to keep his feet moving, but his strength failed and all sensation fled from his massive body. He sprawled on the ground and tried to crawl forward while the awful sound of falling rocks behind him increased to a devilish roar. A cloud of dust enveloped him, and he dimly saw Gedge coming to his aid. Gedge grabbed him and dragged him along the ground. Royston kicked spasmodically with his legs, trying to gain a few more inches toward safety.

Gedge stumbled backward into the main tunnel. He managed to get Royston's head and shoulders clear of the branch tunnel, but a fall of rock came down with a shattering roar and covered the mine owner from the waist down, pinning him to the ground. Gedge staggered back. He looked around for Milligan and saw the miner's inert body nearby. Dust choked Gedge as he turned back to Royston. He saw the pile of rocks covering Royston's legs and thought the mine owner was dead.

But Royston lifted his head and stared up at Gedge, his fleshy face set grimly – desperation showing in his wide eyes. He clawed at the ground in front of him in an effort to get free of the rock fall, but was unable to move.

'For God's sake get me out of here, Gedge!' he shouted, then slumped and lay inert.

Gedge stuck his torch in a crack in the main tunnel and set to work feverishly pulling rocks off Royston. A deadly silence existed now, broken only by an occasional rock falling from the shattered roof. Gedge worked like a maniac until Royston was free. Royston was unconscious, and when Gedge tried to pull him clear of the rock fall he found the mine owner's dead weight was too much for him. He picked up his torch and started back along the main tunnel, intending to get help, leaving Royston in darkness. . . .

Moran began testing the knots in the rope binding him the moment Cullen finished tying them, and soon discovered that he could not hope to get free without help. Cullen left him in a back room and closed the door. Lying on the wooden floor of the room with his hands behind his back, Moran could not exert any pressure on the knots, and sweat beaded his forehead by the time he gave up trying to loosen his bonds. He considered the situation. If he did not get out of this situation then he would surely die, and the information he had gathered about the missing payroll and the murdered soldiers would die with him. But he was bound and helpless, and would surely end up as the escort had – brutally murdered by callous men who cared for nothing but their own selfish ends.

The door of the room was suddenly thrown open and Kenton appeared, manhandling Trooper Davis, whose hands were bound behind his back. Davis was hatless. There was blood and extensive bruising on his face and he was only semi-conscious when Kenton thrust him to the floor beside Moran.

'I told you it was useless trying to get the better of me,' Kenton rasped, chuckling hoarsely. 'I could fight three like you and not raise a sweat. Just you lie there like a good soldier-boy and don't try to give us any more trouble.'

Kenton closed the door. Davis immediately came out of his semi-conscious state, opened his eyes, and gazed alertly at Moran.

'I'm sorry, Captain,' said Davis. 'I didn't have a chance.

I was hit from behind and when I came to I was hogtied. I couldn't get loose, and then that big ox Kenton came in and started to rough me up. I couldn't do anything with my hands tied, except play half-dead. I guess we are gonna be dead in the morning if we can't get the better of them.'

'That's how it looks to me,' said Moran. 'Turn your back to me and I'll try to untie you. If we can get our hands free we might just be able to jump anyone coming back in here. It looks like the only chance we have.'

Davis nodded and twisted around. With his wrists bound tightly, Moran could only move his fingers, and his bonds were tied so tightly he was beginning to lose all sense of feeling in his hands. Unable to see the knots holding Davis, he explored them by touch, and soon discovered that he was unable to loosen them.

'It's no good,' Moran said at length. 'They certainly know how to bind hands together. And the rope is new and stiff. The only way we'd get loose is to use a knife.'

'Let me try to untie you, Captain.'

'Go ahead.' Moran lay motionless while Davis attacked the knots holding him.

'They used old rope on you, sir,' said Davis. 'It's easier to handle, and I think I've got some movement in this knot.'

Moran waited in a fever of anxiety; everything rested on their ability to free themselves. He felt Davis's fingers exerting pressure on the knots and felt a strand of excitement unwinding in his breast. Davis pulled and dragged at the obdurate rope. Moran lay with his ears strained, listening for the ominous sound of someone at the door of the room. Then Davis gave a little cry of triumph.

'Nearly there, Captain,' he said. 'The rope is giving.'

Moran felt the rope suddenly loosen around his wrists. Davis gave a final pull at the knot and Moran was free. He sat up quickly, turned to Davis, and untied the trooper.

'Stay down and pretend you are still bound,' said Moran. He sprang to his feet and crossed to the door, massaging his wrists to get some feeling into them. He stood behind the door, breathing deeply, his eyes glittering as he waited impatiently for one of his captors to make an appearance.

An interminable time passed before Moran heard boots on bare floorboards outside the door. Then a key grated in the lock. The door swung open and Kenton came into the room. Moran swung his right fist the instant he had a clear shot at Kenton's jaw. His bunched knuckles struck Kenton on the chin and the power of the blow sent the big gunman staggering sideways. Moran followed up closely, throwing short-arm punches in rapid succession, hammering Kenton's head and face. The ferocity of the attack bore Kenton to his knees, and Moran paused and kicked viciously with his right foot. The toe of his boot thudded against Kenton's right temple and the big man groaned and sprawled inertly on the floor.

Moran bent and snatched the pistol from Kenton's holster. He cocked the weapon.

'Quickly, Davis; bind him with some of that rope, and make sure he can't get loose. We've got to get out of here.'

Davis sprang up and trussed Kenton. Moran considered his options. There were still three men in the house to be tackled – poor odds for two men with only one gun between them. He went to the window and opened it.

Perhaps it would be wiser to disappear into the night and seek help in the town. He could not afford to lose the initiative now it was firmly in his hands. Then his natural aggressiveness asserted itself and he tightened his grip on the pistol. He checked the weapon and satisfied himself that it was fully loaded. Davis finished binding Kenton and got to his feet.

'Ready when you are, Captain,' he reported.

'We'll go for them,' Moran decided. 'We have surprise on our side. Stay close.'

He turned to the door, opened it carefully and stepped out into a passage. Davis followed and closed the door at his back. The sound of voices came to Moran from the rear of the house and he turned in that direction. He found the door of Floyd's study half open, saw Floyd seated at the desk inside; Ward Price was sitting on a corner of the desk. There was no sign of Cullen. Moran moved in silently. He would feel much happier when Davis had a pistol in his hand. He went in through the doorway and both Floyd and Ward looked up at him, astonishment appearing instantly on their faces. A large pile of wads of paper money lay on the desk – Floyd was in the process of counting it.

'That's the payroll, I assume,' said Moran.

Floyd cursed and his right hand flicked to a drawer in the desk.

'Sit still,' Moran warned, and Floyd curbed his movement.

Ward Price dropped his hand toward the gun at his hip.

'I'd welcome the opportunity to shoot you dead,' Moran said quietly. 'Get your hands up or you'll never come to trial. Davis, get their guns, and then search them thoroughly.'

Davis entered the study as Moran stepped aside in the doorway. He disarmed both men, stuck one pistol in his holster and used the other to cover them.

'Shall we take them back to the jail, Captain?' Davis asked.

'Presently,' said Moran. 'Where is Cullen?'

'Right here, soldier-boy,' said Cullen, and stepped into view in a doorway to the right of the desk.

Moran swung his gun hand, saw Cullen's pistol lifting for a shot and realized that he was at a bad disadvantage. Davis, standing on the far side of Floyd, was not so vulnerable and he fired an instant before Cullen could get his gun into action. His bullet struck Cullen in the right shoulder, the impact spinning the gunman around in the doorway. Cullen fired a shot convulsively, his trigger finger jerking against the curved sliver of steel. Moran jerked as the slug tore into his right forearm. He clenched his teeth as his pistol dropped from his hand. He saw Cullen staggering sideways, but the gunman fired at Davis, and Moran was horrified to see a splotch of blood appear on Davis's forehead between the eyes. Davis fell forward across the desk, knocking against Floyd as he was reaching into a drawer for another gun.

Ward Price sprang up from the desk as Cullen fell to the floor. Moran bent to snatch up his gun, but was unable to use the fingers of his right hand; blood was running from the wound in his forearm. He snatched at the gun with his left hand, and, at that moment, Ward Price jumped him. Moran fell, took a kick in the head and lost his senses in a welter of pain. . . .

Floyd thrust Davis's body off the desk and pulled a gun from the desk drawer.

'Quick, Ward,' Floyd gasped. 'Take a look in that room these two got out of and see what's happened to Kenton. The damn fool must have got careless. I'll watch Moran.'

Ward departed swiftly. Floyd sat on a corner of the desk with his gun covering the inert Moran, his finger trembling on the trigger of the weapon. He was tempted to shoot Moran in cold blood – the man's presence was a great danger. But he hesitated. All the shooting that was going on would bring townsmen hurrying to investigate, and he could not afford to have more witnesses in the town. He glanced down at Davis, saw the bullethole between the soldier's eyes and grunted his satisfaction. At least one of the soldiers was dead.

Kenton came unsteadily into the study and snatched up one of the guns that Davis had dropped. He covered the motionless Moran.

'You want I should kill him?' Kenton demanded, fingering a badly bruised right eye. 'He was waiting for me behind the door when I went into the room, and jumped me.'

'Hold your fire,' Floyd rapped. 'No more shooting. Let's get him and Davis out of here and into the mine before some long-nose comes snooping around to find out what all the shooting was about. Come on, Ward, tie Moran's hands again, and this time make sure he can't get free. Then give Kenton a hand to carry Davis. I'll take care of the big man. We'll dump them in the mine, and tomorrow we'll arrange a burial for them in one of the search tunnels.'

139

Ward fetched rope and trussed Moran, who came back to his senses as he was hauled to his feet. Floyd thrust the muzzle of his pistol under his nose.

'The first sign of any more trouble from you and I'll shoot you between the eyes,' he warned.

Moran braced his knees in order to stay on his feet. He watched Kenton and Ward Price pick up Davis's lifeless body and carry it to the back door, and he had no option but to follow when Floyd jabbed him in the back with the muzzle of his pistol. They left the house and walked slowly uphill toward the silent mine. . . .

TEN

Kerry Talmadge drank steadily for an hour, his thoughts flitting over the broad spectrum of the situation confronting him. The longer he considered Floyd Price's attitude the more convinced he became that Floyd was planning to double-cross him as soon as Royston departed from Moundville. He set down his glass and slammed his right hand on the table top, spilling Frint's drink.

'Now what the hell is wrong?' demanded Frint. 'You look like you've reached your limit for the night. Come on. I'll see you up to your room.'

'No!' Kerry leaned his elbows on the table. 'Listen to me, Frint. I've been thinking, and I don't like what has come to mind. I believe that when Royston departs tomorrow, Floyd will try to gyp me out of the mine and take over himself.'

'Don't tell me you're getting some sense at last!' Frint grinned. 'Hell, I've been telling you for the last fortnight that Floyd will skin you alive when he thinks the time is right. Now you've worked it out for yourself, huh? So what are you gonna do about Floyd? Do you want me to shoot him?'

'The hell I do! Are you forgetting the payroll? I need that dough, and Floyd will be safe until I get my hands on it.'

'He's got to start spending it the minute Royston pulls out,' said Frint. 'That's tomorrow. So you won't have long to wait, and I'll shoot Floyd the minute you get the dough.'

'I'd like to find some way of stopping work at the mine until I've had a good chance to work out what I really want to do,' mused Kerry.

'There's only one thing that will stop work in a gold-mine and that's a cave-in.' Frint grimaced. 'I'm good with a gun but I don't know a thing about dynamite except that it can blow you to bits.'

'Miners would soon dig out a cave-in.' Kerry's eyes glinted. 'Do you recall what happened when Bonanza was flooded a few months ago? Everything came to a standstill. Floyd had to find out where the water came from. It was that mountain stream up in the hills.'

'He diverted the stream,' said Cass, 'so it can't flood the mine again.'

'I know that. I saw the place where a dam was built. But what if the dam was dynamited? The mine would be flooded for a couple of months at least. Now there's a thought. Let's take a stroll along the street and look in the saloons. I need to find that miner who has got a grudge against Royston and was fired from the mine last month. I think he might be persuaded to do a job for me.'

'Yeah, I remember him,' said Cass. 'I offered to shoot him for fifty dollars but Royston wouldn't go for it.'

'His name is Goymer. I saw him working in that little

bar just past the bank. Come on, let's talk to him.'

Frint shrugged but made no comment. Kerry led the way out of the hotel and they walked through the shadows on the street to the small bar. There were half a dozen customers inside and Kerry's eyes gleamed when he saw the ex-miner serving drinks behind the bar. He walked to the bar and leaned an elbow on it. Goymer was tall and heavily built, with thick black brows over narrowed brown eyes. He had a square chin that jutted pugnaciously. His scowling expression deepened when he recognized Kerry.

'What do you want in this end of the town?' Goymer demanded. 'Have they run out of drink at the hotel?'

'Is this the way you welcome customers?' asked Kerry.

'Only the one who has a father called Royston Talmadge,' replied Goymer.

'As I remember it your disagreement wasn't with my father,' said Kerry. 'It was Floyd who fired you.'

'And Floyd works for your father – the big boss. So what do you want? You look like you've had enough to drink already, so I ain't likely to serve you.'

'I want to talk to you,' said Kerry.

'Yeah?' Suspicion showed in Goymer's dark eyes. 'What gives?'

'I'll tell you somewhere less public.'

'Come into the back room.' Goymer led the way to a door at the rear of the saloon and Kerry accompanied him, leaving Frint at the bar. 'So what's on your mind?' Goymer asked as he closed the door behind Kerry.

'I've heard you were making threats against Bonanza,' said Kerry. 'Was it just wild talk or would you really hit at the mine and earn some dough for doing it?'

'What are you trying on?' Goymer frowned. 'The Bonanza belongs to your father. You wouldn't want to harm his business.'

'How much would it take to get you to place a charge of dynamite against the dam Floyd built to divert the mountain stream that flooded the mine earlier this year?'

Goymer's eyes widened. They looked like black stones from a creek bed.

'You want to flood the mine again? Why?'

'The reason is not important. Tell me how much you'd ask to do the job?'

Goymer gazed at Kerry's smiling face. He moistened his lips and swallowed noisily.

'I reckon it would set you back a hundred bucks.'

'Let's say half now, and the rest when the job is done.' Kerry reached into his pocket and produced a black leather wallet; he opened it, and took out a thin wad of notes. 'Fifty dollars,' he said, counting off the sum and handing it over. 'You can pick up the rest from me at the hotel in the morning.'

'When do you want the job done?'

'Before the morning shift goes in at four. I don't want any of the miners killed.'

'Where do I get the dynamite from?'

Kerry smiled. 'You know where dynamite is stored at the mine as well as I do,' he responded. 'You're an experienced miner, so go and help yourself.'

'I can get the job done an hour after the shift comes off,' said Goymer. 'Will that do?'

'That will be fine. I'll look forward to giving you the rest of the dough in the morning.'

Goymer opened the door and Kerry departed. Kerry motioned to Frint and they left the bar. . . .

Matt Gedge gasped with relief when he emerged from the mine and breathed fresh air. He ran through the shadows to the hut where the night watchman had his quarters. Faint yellow lamplight emanated from the window of the building and he lunged at the door and burst into the hut. The night watchman was sitting asleep at a table, his head in his hands. Gedge grasped his shoulder and shook him roughly.

'Jackson, wake up. Come and give me a hand to get Royston Talmadge out of the mine. There's been a cave-in.'

Jackson started up out of his chair in shock, and reached for the gun he was wearing in a holster on his right hip. He gazed blearily at Gedge, his eyes filled with sleep.

'What the hell!' he demanded. 'You got no call to come busting in here like that. What do you want?'

Gedge sighed impatiently. He paused to give Jackson time to collect his wits.

'The big boss is down in the mine and he's hurt,' said Gedge. 'I want you to come and give me a hand to get him up to the surface. There's been a cave-in, and more of the roof is likely to go, so we've got no time to lose.'

Jackson cursed and picked up a coiled rope. 'I should report to the mine manager before I do anything,' he said.

'There's no time for that. We must get the boss out.'

Jackson grumbled and protested all the way back to the mine entrance but did not refuse to enter. He picked up a torch, set it burning and led the way down to the lower level. When they reached the spot where Royston was lying, the mine owner looked up at them. His was face streaked with dirt, his body covered with dust.

'What took you so long, Gedge?' demanded Royston. 'So you're the watchman, Jackson! I'll bet you were asleep up there. If you weren't snoring you would have heard the cave-in. Come on, get me out of this. I think my left leg is broken. How are you gonna get me to the surface?'

'I'd better go for more help,' said Jackson. 'What's been going on down here?' He looked in the direction of the motionless Milligan. Who is that stretched out over there? Is he dead?'

'Cut out the questions and give me a hand to get up,' snapped Royston.

'You won't be able to walk with a broken leg,' opined Gedge.

'I said I think it is broken,' growled Royston, 'so get me up and we'll find out! Stop making excuses and set to work. Jackson, you'll lose your job if you don't heave me to my feet.'

'We'll need half a dozen men to get you to the surface,' protested Jackson. 'I know what I'm talking about. I've helped to get more injured men out of this mine than you've had hot dinners, Boss. Let me go fetch some help. It will be quicker that way.'

'Damn you!' roared Royston. 'Get me out of this tunnel. The roof has just collapsed. Take me to the bottom of the entrance shaft where it will be safer, and then go for help if you've a mind to.'

'You take one side of him and I'll take the other,' said

Gedge. 'Come on, Jackson. Let's get him on his feet. We'll soon discover if he's got a broken leg.'

Between them they hauled Royston to his feet. Royston put weight on his left leg and tested it gingerly.

'I think it's OK,' he gasped. 'I can stand on it. But it hurts like hell. Come on; let's get out of here.'

They began to stagger along the tunnel toward the vertical shaft. Royston rested most of his great weight on the shoulders of Gedge and Jackson. They almost collapsed under him, but made slow progress. They had almost reached the shaft and were pausing for a breather, when Jackson hissed at them.

'Listen!' he said. 'Someone is coming.'

They fell silent. Dim torchlight showed above them from the top of the shaft.

'Quick!' Royston gasped. 'Jackson, I don't want anyone to know I'm down here. Have you got that? Go up and tell whoever is up there that you heard the cave-in and came down to investigate. Lead them away from here and come back for me later. Gedge, get me into a branch tunnel and we'll lie low. Jackson, do this right or you're out of a job.'

'Who's down there?' a voice called from above.

'That's Floyd's voice.' whispered Gedge. 'Come this way, Boss. Jackson, get up that ladder. We'll see you later.'

Jackson moved off, taking the torch with him. Gedge helped Royston back the way they had come and they eased into the mouth of a branch tunnel as darkness closed in around them. They could faintly hear Jackson's voice as he reported to Floyd.

'Was the cave-in in the tunnel with the danger sign across its entrance?' demanded Floyd.

'Yeah, that's the one,' replied Jackson. 'It looks like it has collapsed all the way out from the face to the main tunnel. Say, who is that with you, and why is he hogtied? What the hell is going on around here tonight?'

'Get out of here and mind your business,' rasped Floyd. 'We caught this guy trying to break into Royston's house so we are gonna hold him until the morning because we can't find the deputy sheriff to jail him. Beat it, Jackson. Go back to sleep in your hut.'

'What is that all about?' Royston said in a hoarse undertone. 'Who have they got hogtied up there?'

'We shall soon find out,' said Gedge. 'They are coming down to this level.'

Several voices sounded as Moran was lowered down the shaft on the end of a rope. Gedge peered along the main tunnel as Kenton descended the ladder carrying a torch and watched as Moran was half dragged into a branch tunnel nearer the shaft.

'We'll be back to finish you off in the morning,' Kenton said as he departed. He stuck the torch in a crevice and ascended the ladder.

'Unhook the top section of the ladder in case he gets free before morning,' said Floyd. 'He's got the better of us too many times tonight.'

'I hope it isn't Kerry they've got hold of,' said Royston.

'Hang on a minute and we'll find out,' responded Gedge, as he heard the sound of a ladder being dragged up out of the shaft.

Full silence returned and Royston moved impatiently.

'Take a look at who was brought down here,' he ordered.

Gedge slipped into the main tunnel and walked towards the vertical shaft. He looked into the branch tunnel and saw Moran lying trussed on the rock floor. A body dressed in a soldier's uniform was motionless beside Moran.

'Who are you, feller?' asked Gedge. 'Why has Floyd Price dumped you in here?'

'I'm Provost Captain Moran, investigating an army payroll robbery and the murder of its escort. Untie me, please, and then loan me a gun. I need to make some arrests.'

'So why did Floyd take you prisoner? Was he involved in the robbery?'

Moran gave a brief account of the events leading to his incarceration in the mine. Gedge listened in silence, and began untying Moran before he had learned all the facts.

'I've got Royston Talmadge, the mine owner, back there,' said Gedge. 'If you give me a hand to get him to the surface, I'll help you grab Floyd and his brother.'

Moran sighed with relief as his bonds slackened.

'Who killed the soldier?' asked Gedge.

'Cullen.'

'One of Floyd's troubleshooters, and I heard Kenton's voice when he brought you down. So they are all involved, huh?' Gedge led the way back to where Royston was sitting in the branch tunnel, and explained the situation to his boss.

'There's no end to the skulduggery that's been going on under my nose,' cursed Royston. 'I'm glad to make your acquaintance, Captain. Give me a hand to get up to the surface and we'll help you get the men you want. We are in the process of thwarting a plot to steal this mine from me, and the men you want seem to be involved in my trouble. Let's get out of here and we'll give them a taste of justice.'

Moran was in pain from the bullet wound he had sustained in his right forearm but he helped Gedge haul Royston to his feet and moved on to the vertical shaft. Kenton had left a torch burning at the entrance to the branch tunnel in which Moran had been dumped and Gedge fetched it. He held it high to inspect the vertical shaft.

'I heard Floyd tell Kenton to remove the top section of the ladder,' Gedge said, 'and it is gone. They've taken out the top ten feet. So how do we get up there?'

'Jackson will be back shortly,' said Royston. He sat down beside the foot of the bottom section of the ladder. 'He'll put the ladder back in place and we'll climb out.'

Moran took the torch, ascended ten feet up the ladder to its limit, and found another ten feet of smooth bare rock stretching above his head to the upper level. There was no possible way to get higher without the section of ladder which had been removed. He returned to the bottom of the shaft and reported what he had seen.

'So we wait for Jackson to return,' said Royston. 'He'd better not keep me waiting long or he'll be out of a job. I can't wait to see Floyd's face when we confront him. Are you sure he was involved in the payroll robbery, Captain?'

'He didn't take part in the robbery but planned it with his brother Ward, who was a soldier with the payroll escort, and as far as I can ascertain, Floyd's three troubleshooters were involved. There were other soldiers involved, but only Ward Price survived the shooting.'

'Say, what is that noise?' cut in Gedge. 'It sounds like running water!'

Moran heard the sound at that moment – a roaring, gushing noise, like a great volume of water swirling through a gorge.

'It is running water!' he said sharply.

Royston grasped the rungs of the ladder and began to haul himself to his feet.

'The mine was flooded some months ago!' he said. 'A mountain stream broke through into the end of this tunnel, and it sounds like it has done so again. Get as high as you can.'

Royston began to climb the ladder with difficulty. Gedge tried to assist his boss without success. Moran held the torch high. The roaring sound increased in volume, and suddenly a three-foot wave of water came surging towards them from the rift in the rocks at the end of the main tunnel. Being prevented from continuing down the rift by the boards placed across the floor of the tunnel, the descending water was rapidly finding its own level. Moran grasped the side of the ladder as the wave struck them and then surged upwards into the vertical shaft. He was immediately immersed over his head, and almost lost his grasp on the ladder as the wave receded, pulling at him with its surging vortex. He reached out, grabbed at Gedge as the man slipped and was almost washed away, but held on to Gedge's arm as the wave receded. Then a second wave, larger than the first, came surging back toward them. The depth of water increased rapidly as the tunnel filled with the endless torrent rushing down from the dynamited dam.

Royston reached the upper limit of the ladder and slid an arm over the top rung. Moran and Gedge clung to the sides of the ladder and ascended as the water rose around them. By degrees the force of the rising water lessened as it levelled out, and settled when it reached up to Royston's knees. The sound of water gushing away somewhere in the darkness was the only sound in the darkened mine. Moran clung to the ladder and hung on desperately. Gedge cursed as he hung on to the ladder on the other side of Royston.

'That was a damn near thing!' exclaimed Royston. 'Where in hell is Jackson? He should be back here by now.'

'Let us hope Floyd didn't hear the sound of the water coming in and returns to investigate,' observed Gedge. 'If he does show up and sticks his head over the edge up there I'll put a slug through his scheming brain.'

'There's someone moving around up there now,' observed Royston.

They remained silent; listening intently. Faint sounds came down to them from the upper level.

'Don't call out,' warned Moran. 'It could be Floyd and his friends returning, and they'll start shooting if they find us down here.'

'The hell with it,' growled Royston. 'I want out of here.' He raised his voice and called urgently: 'Who's up there? Put the ladder back in place and help me out of here.'

'There's someone down there,' a voice said.

Moran's hopes were dashed when he recognized Kenton's voice. Faint light illuminated the shaft as a blazing torch was held out over it. Moran immediately loosed his hold on the ladder and swam to one side. He could see Royston peering anxiously upward.

'The main tunnel is flooded,' said Kenton, 'and someone is clinging to the ladder.'

'I recognized the voice,' said Floyd. 'I'll be damned if it isn't Royston!'

'Get me out of here,' yelled Royston. 'I was on an inspection tour when the roof of a branch tunnel collapsed on me, and then the mine flooded. Get me out but quick.'

Moran eased further away from the ladder. He saw two heads appear over the edge of the shaft.

'So you couldn't resist the temptation to stick your nose in down there, huh?' demanded Floyd. 'What did you find? Did you see that new strike I made?'

'I saw enough to know that you are a lowdown, thieving four-flusher, you scheming sidewinder,' yelled Royston.

Moran clenched his teeth, aware of what would happen next.

'Are you down there on your own?' demanded Floyd.

'I am,' bluffed Royston. 'I know what's been going on, Floyd, and I suspect that you led Kerry astray in this steal you've plotted.'

Moran pressed his left hand against the smooth wall of the shaft and kicked his feet to remain afloat. He caught a movement above his head as Royston fell silent. The next instant a pistol hammered and red-orange flame spurted from its muzzle. The crash of two shots sounded enormously loud in the close confines of the tunnel. Royston fell off the ladder and disappeared under the surface of the water as Floyd laughed mockingly.

'I've waited years to put a slug in you, Royston,' he

153

shouted. 'Now I'll deal with Kerry.'

The echoes of the shots faded and silence returned as Moran dived away from the shaft wall, his hands outstretched to grasp Royston. He caught hold of a massive shoulder and kicked powerfully with his legs to drag the massive bulk of the mine owner back to the surface. Moran's head broke surface in time to see the torchlight disappearing from the top of the shaft. He eased back to the ladder, taking Royston with him, and grasped a wooden rung as a hand came out of the darkness and gabbed his arm.

'They've done for Royston,' said Gedge. 'He should have kept quiet. I can't swim. Have you got Royston?'

'Yes, but I don't know if he's alive or dead. I'll hold him while you check him.'

A moment passed and water splashed. 'Hey, he's still breathing!' exclaimed Gedge. 'It would take more than a rat like Floyd to finish off Royston. But we've got to get out of here before Floyd kills Kerry Talmadge.'

'There is no way out without help,' observed Moran. 'We need that watchman.'

They clung to the ladder, holding Royston afloat between them, and waited in silence. Time seemed to stand still. The water was freezing, and a deadly inertia began to take hold of Moran. Then, after what seemed an eternity, a dim light appeared in the upper tunnel and a worried voice called from above.

'Are you still there, Boss? This is Jackson.'

'For God's sake get the top section of the ladder back in place, Jackson,' called Gedge. 'We can't hold on much longer. This water is freezing.'

Moran heard noises – wood scraping against rock and the click of metal against metal.

'OK,' called Jackson at length. 'The ladder is back on. Come on up.'

'Lower a rope so we can haul Royston up. He's been shot. And stick a couple of torches up so we can see what we're doing.'

The top of the shaft was illuminated and a rope came snaking down to where they were clinging. Moran passed the end of the rope under Royston's arms and knotted it across his chest. Gedge ascended first and hauled on the rope to keep Royston's head above water. Moran ascended the ladder and they hauled on the rope, bringing the mine owner up the shaft and pulling him on to solid ground like a gigantic fish. Moran examined Royston and found him breathing. There was a bullet wound in the top of Royston's right shoulder and an exit wound in his shoulder blade.

'I think he'll live,' Moran said.

'Jackson, fetch the doctor and be quick about it.' Gedge pulled a gun from the holster under his armpit and checked it. 'We'd better get moving,' he rasped. 'Floyd will kill Kerry.'

'I need a gun,' said Moran.

'Give him yours, Jackson.' Gedge began to move toward the entrance of the mine.

Jackson unbuckled his cartridge belt and held it out to Moran, who threw it across his left shoulder as he ran after the fast-moving Gedge. Moran drew the pistol from its holster, paused beside the flickering torches at the mine entrance and checked the weapon. He went on, conscious of pain in his right arm, but held the pistol grimly and ran to catch up with Gedge. They neared Royston's house. Lamplight was flaring from several ground floor windows, and Moran saw three figures standing at a front corner, silhouetted against the glare, with two other figures confronting them.

'That's Kerry and Frint with Floyd,' hissed Gedge. 'What are they saying?'

Kerry's voice came to them on the cool night air.

'I want the payroll money, Floyd,' Kerry said. 'You're out of this now. You were figuring to double-cross me, but I've got in first.'

'You are a stupid skunk, Kerry!' replied Floyd. 'The stakes are higher than you thought. Royston is dead back there in the mine and the whole game is changed. I suppose you had the dam dynamited, huh? Well, I've dried it out before and I can do it again.'

'You're finished,' Kerry responded. 'Kill them, Frint.'

Floyd, Ward and Kenton opened fire immediately and Kerry and Frint responded. Gun echoes hammered and flashes tore through the gloom. Kenton dived off to the right but did not stop shooting. Ward Price went down on one knee and his gun stopped firing. Floyd stood his ground and triggered his gun desperately, afraid now that all his plans were coming unstitched. He aimed for Frint, knowing the gunman was more deadly than Kerry, and he saw Frint suddenly fall forward on to his face. He swung his muzzle to cover Kerry Talmadge, but Kerry was finished; Kenton was pumping slug after slug into the youngster.

Moran saw Kerry and Frint go down, and the shooting

ceased abruptly. Kenton got quickly to his feet. Ward sprang up from cover and made for the corner of the house.

'That does it,' yelled Floyd. 'We're in the clear now.'

'Not yet!' shouted Gedge. 'This is clean-up time, Floyd. Royston is still alive, no thanks to you, and I'm here to settle his debts.'

Floyd and Kenton turned quickly and again gunfire hammered; spurts of flame lanced through the night. Moran ducked a whining slug that came close to catching him and triggered his borrowed gun. He wanted Ward Price alive, if possible, and caught a glimpse of him pausing at the corner of the house as he threw lead at Gedge. Kenton was beside Floyd, and they fired indiscriminately into the shadows, intent on killing all opposition.

Moran dropped to one knee as two more slugs breathed on him in passing. He concentrated on Ward Price, snapped two shots in quick succession, and saw Ward duck back out of sight around the corner. Floyd redoubled his efforts, firing a string of shots at Gedge's muzzle flame. Kenton had stopped shooting and was staggering around, trying to get his gun into action but failing. Moran fired at Kenton and saw him pitch sideways to the ground and lie still. Gedge triggered his gun and stitched three slugs into Floyd's chest. Floyd fell away. The shooting ceased then and an uneasy silence replaced it.

Gedge went toward the corner of the big house. Lamplight from a nearby window shone upon the figures sprawled on the ground. Moran went to Floyd Price and bent over him. Floyd was breathing, but only just. Moran dropped to one knee beside the man. He saw blood soaking the front of his shirt. Floyd coughed harshly and blood spurted from his mouth. He tried to speak but could only make an animal sound. Then he trembled violently and stiffened. The breath left his body in a long, drawn-out sigh as he relaxed in death.

'Floyd's dead,' observed Moran, getting to his feet.

'So is Kenton,' said Gedge, moving on to where Kerry Talmadge and Frint were lying. 'They killed Kerry and Frint before we could stop them. What happened to the third man who was here? He took off pretty damn quick. Does this wind up your business, Captain?'

'No.' Moran shook his head. 'I want Ward Price, and I think I know where he has gone. I'll go and pick him up.'

'Do you need any more help?' asked Gedge.

'No thanks.' Moran checked his gun and reloaded the empty chambers in the cylinder.

'I'd better get back to Royston then.' Gedge turned away. 'We'll check with you later, huh?'

'I shall be around,' promised Moran.

'And the mine is still safe,' observed Gedge. 'Floyd sure was playing for high stakes.'

'They committed murder to take the payroll,' observed Moran, 'and died trying to keep it.'

'Where is the payroll?' asked Gedge.

'It was down in Floyd's house when I saw it earlier.' Moran straightened. 'I expect Ward has gone to collect it.'

Gedge turned and went swiftly back up to the mine. Moran set off down the hill and the strong mountain breeze blew the last clinging tendrils of gunsmoke out of his nostrils. He moved swiftly through the shadows, intent now on taking Ward Price. He clutched the gun in his right hand, heedless of the pain he was getting from the wound in his arm. He approached Floyd's house from the rear. Lamplight was shining from the window of Floyd's study and Moran moved in to peer through the window. He saw a short, fleshy man standing beside Floyd's desk; both his hands were clutching wads of paper money. Ward Price was standing in the doorway of the room, a levelled pistol in his right hand.

Moran hurried around the house to the front door, which was standing ajar. He entered and made for the study. A gun blasted as he reached the doorway, and he peered into the study to see the man at the desk fall face down upon the payroll. Ward Price started forward to the desk, but sensed he was not alone and came swinging around, his eyes wide and his mouth agape. He threw up his gun hand. The weapon exploded before it could level at Moran, and the bullet ploughed into the door jamb beside Moran's left ear. Gunsmoke plumed across the room. Ward changed his position quickly. The muzzle of Moran's gun followed him, and blasted fire and smoke as Ward tried to work his pistol.

Ward took Moran's bullet in the centre of his chest. He dropped his gun and fell back over the desk. Blood dribbled from his wound to stain the money he had murdered to get. Moran kicked Ward's gun into a corner and then checked his man. Ward was dead. He had cheated the hangman but paid the forfeit for failure.

Moran checked the stranger stretched across the desk, unaware that it was Bodeen, the banker. There were still many questions Moran needed answering, but he knew enough to pin the blame where it belonged, and he was satisfied. . . .